PRAISE

"Like any good fairytale, enjoyed over a cup of chamomile tea by a winter fire, this short book delights with dark woods, perilous quests, animal familiars, and kindly strangers, but its simplicity is deceptive, and it soon weaves into a gentle meditation on worlds Old and New, on losses big and small, and on the gift of human connection, both familial and fleeting. One of the most moving stories I have read in recent years."

~ Olga Grushin, author of *The Dream Life of Sukhanov*

"A deeply moving and tense look into the lives of immigrants in America and Europe at the dawn of the twentieth century. Jaskunas gives us a heartbreaking, exhilarating story of two countries and one divided family. Written with acute observation, this is a beautifully told tale of separation, hardship, and longing that will move and enthrall. I loved these people and never wanted to leave them."

~ Edward Carey, author of *Little* and *The Swallowed Man*

PRAISE FOR *THE ATLAS OF REMEDIES*

"This propulsive, cross-continental adventure story about the boundlessness of familial love beguiles and surprises. Paul Jaskunas's writing is gorgeous and precise, and his affection for these characters illuminates every page. *The Atlas of Remedies* is a dazzling accomplishment."

~ Michelle Ross, author of *Shapeshifting*

"*The Atlas of Remedies*, an historical novella by Paul Jaskunas, is set in 1901, yet it is mirrored daily by globally displaced people. Karolina, an anxious mother abandoned by her husband, immigrates from Russian-ruled Lithuania to Manhattan to find work while her children, Lukas and Ona, embark on their own journey to find their mother. Jaskunas reminds us that immigration stories, like those of our own families, are important tales with common cause to collectively weave our threads into the larger cloth, the greater American story. Add this one to the list for your book club."

~ Robert Miltner, author of
Orpheus & Echo and *Ohio Apertures*

THE ATLAS OF REMEDIES
PAUL JASKUNAS

STILL
HOUSE
PRESS

Copyright © 2024 by Paul Jaskunas

FIRST EDITION

All rights reserved.

No part of this book may be reproduced without written permission from the publisher.

All inquiries may be directed to:

Stillhouse Press

4400 University Drive, 3E4

Fairfax, VA 22030

www.stillhousepress.org

Excerpts from this work originally appeared in *The Museum of Americana*

Stillhouse Press is an independent, student- and alumni-run nonprofit press based out of Northern Virginia and operated in collaboration with Watershed Lit: Center for Literary Engagement and Publishing Practice at George Mason University.

Library of Congress Control Number: 2023947239

ISBN-13: 978-1-945233-24-1

Jacket Design and Back Image: Christopher Kardambikis
Interior Images: Lukas Jaskunas
Interior Design: Paul Logan IV

This book is for my children, Dainora and Lukas

I

One black dawn in the winter of 1901, the children's uncle rose to hunt. The boy, in bed, waited until he could no longer hear the sound of the man's boots breaking the crust of snow in the yard. Then he looked at his older sister Ona, who slept beside him in bed. He could see her breath in the air. Their uncle had neglected to start the fire, so Lukas crept into the kitchen and, as quietly as he could, placed split logs of pine into the ashy stove. She kept on sleeping as he lit the fire and built it up fierce and hot. If he made the house warm enough, she wouldn't wake from the cold, and he could slip away unseen.

He stretched and kicked the stove door closed with his bare foot. Through the grate, the flames made soft shadows leap on the wall. By their light, he could see the remains of his uncle's breakfast—a half-eaten sausage and a hunk of black bread. He sliced these thinly with a knife and ate them together, stuffing his mouth and chewing fast as he knelt before the stove to warm himself. He watched the flames through the grate in a trance, fixing in his mind the wide orbit of the sun swinging over New York, shining upon his mother's shoulders. Holding an apple in one hand, an egg in another, his sister had explained to him the mystery of the sun being two places at once. Still, it wasn't easy to grasp the simultaneity of his dawn and his mother's noon.

He dressed in silence, in his warmest clothes, his coat, and boots. Avoiding the creaky boards in the floor, he went to a high shelf and stood on a stool to reach a Jesus figurine carved from oak. Inside its hollow core, he found a small purse of leather. He spilled three coins into his hand and pocketed them. Then he went into the cold, closing the wood door gently.

The forest loomed across the yard. He paused before it, considering the dark spaces between trees. As he began to walk, the sound of the snow breaking under his boots gave him courage.

It was four kilometers to the village. The way would take him through long stretches of forest and marshland now trapped in ice. Tall pines with cinnamon-colored trunks held snow in their branches. Invisible creatures had inscribed the white forest floor with ink-like tracings. Elk roamed these woods, and his uncle was hunting them even now, at first light, when every twig and log looked touched by the grace of a wintery god. Lukas had walked long enough to feel the cold in his toes when he heard the first shot echo through the pines.

There would be a corpse in the yard tonight. The children would be expected to strip the hide and butcher the meat amid a hot glut of gore. He'd rather eat old potatoes all winter than confront the bloodied face of the elk.

Lukas pressed on, faster now.

In time, he came to the bridge that crossed the frozen Merkys. Here he paused at the apex and looked down to the scrim of ice, the blur of quick water beneath, and there the sand empurpled by silt and shadow. Downstream, the river widened and fed the marsh that teemed with frogs. In summer, he'd come here once with his mother to swim. He'd been too light for the current. It would have swept him away from her, but she'd held him in the river, her hands upon his waist, under his arms. She'd turned him over so he could look up at her as the water sluiced around him. He'd laughed softly and she'd said, good, you can swim, see? Even little Lukas can swim.

He walked a long way, along the white river, toward the village. As he walked, he thought of his mother's face. He wanted to remember it exactly, to hold in his mind the slope of her nose, the pale birthmark on her left temple, and the soft blonde down over her lip. He missed her so badly he had resolved to draw her. In the village, he would buy paper and pencil.

It was a mere gathering of wood houses, barns, a store, and a white church with a tall steeple. Its altar, carved from birch, had been paid for with dollars sent by those living now in America—people who perhaps would never see their home again. Many houses were empty—their owners had left the yards heaped with snow and the chimneys cold. The largest home, the rectory behind the church, had been taken by the Czar's police; the priest, Father Rambauskas, a family friend, had been deported to Siberia. One officer stumbled now across the yard to the outhouse. He wore boots and a nightshirt. Lukas waited for him to go inside.

There were eight of these men stationed in the village. The peasants called them Cossacks, though they did not know their ethnicity for certain. They'd come here because the village had broken the law. A school in the church cellar had taught children to read Lithuanian—an illegal activity under Russian rule. Then a man had been caught smuggling nationalist newspapers into the country, and the village priest was found to have owned a library of banned Lithuanian-language books. The Cossacks had burned every last printed page, exiled the priest, and jailed the smuggler. They had little more to do here, but they stayed on, practicing their shooting and exercising their horses in a pasture behind the store. Sometimes these beasts were left to frolic along the river, and the children, in summer, had enjoyed watching them graze and run, frightening the storks that stalked the banks for food.

Lukas had an apple in his pocket. He took it out as he walked to the stables. The horses stood in their stalls, presenting long stoic faces. He came to his favorite, an auburn mare he'd named Cherry. She reached out with bare teeth and took the apple from his hand. Her head swung happily upward as she chomped, spraying juice.

His mother had once owned a mare the color of honey. Lukas had only a dim memory of this creature, but his sister Ona, now fourteen, had learned to ride her. Their father had sold the horse on the sly to help pay for his ticket to America, to escape conscription into the Czar's army. He'd been gone five years now. Not once had his offspring heard from him. Was the man alive? Did he think of his children? Lukas only knew that his father had taken the family's horse and never come back.

The boy heard behind him the clink of metal. The Cossack he'd seen earlier had come into the stable. He was a bearded man; he carried tackle in his hands.

—What do you want with the horse, boy?

He spoke Russian, a language Lukas knew but not yet very well. He tried to think of the right words to answer.

—I gave it an apple.

—It's already had its breakfast.

Lukas looked at the Cossack's boots.

—Look at me.

Lukas looked up.

—You want a whipping?

Lukas tried to scamper away through the door, but the officer caught him by his coat collar and jerked him off his feet; he fell to his knees.

—Don't come bothering my horse again, the man grumbled, pushing the boy into the snow.

Lukas bolted to his feet and ran as fast as he could to the store, glancing behind him once to see if the officer was chasing after him. He'd already disappeared into the shadows of the barn.

The village shop was closed, the owner asleep, so Lukas banged on the window of the bedroom until the old man got out of bed. He stood naked in the room. His skin sagged from his ribs and arms. He had thick white hair. People said he had half his wits left, meaning it as a compliment, for he was old enough to remember Napoleon's army. He came to the door now with leggings and a wool sweater and ushered the boy into the shop.

Here were oak barrels stocked with flour, barley, birch sap, and molasses, and on the shelves, bottles of medicines, potions, and teas.

—I want to buy paper, he said in Lithuanian.

The old man went behind the counter and pulled out a wooden box. He showed the boy two packets, and the boy chose the more expensive—thick paper with an eggshell tint. He also bought a pencil he would use to draw with and at once began to sharpen it with his pocket knife.

—Are there any letters for us?

—No.

—Are you sure?

—You think I wouldn't tell you with your mother in America? She wrote last month, didn't she?

—Yes.

—So? She is fine. Of course, Karolina's fine. Why do you worry?

Lukas didn't answer. A month was a long time. Before that letter, they'd had word about every two weeks for half a year. Her notes were short, the ink often smudged with weather, but they understood she'd crossed in good health and that New York was dazzling and crowded and wild. She'd written of novelties—the scent of lemons, buildings taller than any hillside, a man who played trumpet on a rooftop at sundown. No word yet of work or dollars. It was like their mother to write around the subject of greatest importance.

—Will you send someone to tell us when the next letter comes? the boy asked the shopkeeper.

—Of course. When it comes. It could take time. She may have left New York. There are other cities. So many cities there—a country full of cities. Why did she leave us? What is money? It has no use in heaven. I told your mother to stay, she didn't listen. Now she's in a strange place full of noise, and we wait for word. I'm sorry, my boy.

Lukas didn't want to hear anymore. The shopkeeper couldn't understand what it was to have nothing—no land and no prospects. For years now, Lukas, Ona, and their mother Karolina had relied on the meager generosity of the boy's uncle, the missing father's eldest brother, who'd inherited the family's tiny farm. He fed, housed, and clothed them, but did so grudgingly and resented his younger brother for leaving his brood behind. For his part, Lukas despised his uncle. His manners were rude, and he'd scold or beat the children at the slightest transgression.

These conditions ought not have come to pass. The children ought to have been wealthy, for Karolina's ancestors had, not long ago, been rich landowners. As a reckless young man, however, her Polish grandfather had lost their estate to gambling debts. Once her husband abandoned her, the children's mother could count on nothing but the stipend the priest had offered her to teach in the underground school. As soon as she'd saved enough, she'd left for America, promising to send for Ona and Lukas as soon as she could pay their passage. Villagers had tried to dissuade her from going so far away, but she insisted. She didn't want to live any longer with her in-law or, for that matter, under the Russians, who would conscript her son as soon as he was of age. Anyway, America promised a freer life. Her cousin Marija's letters, after all, had raved of the marvels of New York.

Lukas spilled the stolen coins onto a wooden counter. He put his paper and pencil inside his coat pocket and politely thanked the shopkeeper.

—You will come to mass on Sunday, the old man asked?

—Yes, he said, going out the door.

Lukas stood in the yard and blinked. He held the paper tightly in his coat. In the distance, he saw the auburn mare, the Cossack upon her back riding high over white fields.

When he returned home, Ona and their uncle were busy in the back with the elk. It hung from a rope tied round its neck and thrown over a stout branch. It had been cut open, from sternum to anus, and flaps of the hide dripped blood into the snow, melting it. The silky red organs steamed in a puddle beneath. The boy could smell them, the wet musk of fresh guts. He paused to consider the crumpled grimace of the elk, the frozen and senseless eyes, then walked quietly to the door, escaping notice.

Inside, alone, he went to his bed in the room beside the kitchen. He tore open the paper and began to draw.

The sensation of lead on thick paper calmed him at once. He missed going to school, writing and drawing. His mother, who'd been educated from a young age, had been his teacher, along with the exiled priest. But now the village school was shut down and there was nowhere nearby to go. He closed his eyes and pictured his mother's face as she'd held him in the Merkys that day they'd swam near the bridge. He wanted to get that look, that smile. He drew well, but not well enough to give life to eyes drawn in lead. Each mark he made disappointed. As he drew in her eyebrows, he wondered what she might be doing in the great city. They'd never seen a photograph of New York so he could only imagine what it looked like. A man from the village had gone to live there long ago and came back with stories of streets full of more people than you could imagine—rivers of people, flowing more swiftly than the Merkys after a hard rain. Where were all these people going? To do what? Lukas had the impression that New Yorkers were giants. He worried his mother would be outsized, overrun; it would be hard for her to keep up with the great strides of so many large men.

He finished her eyes. Flat on the empty page, they didn't look like hers. He sighed and gripped the pencil and began to outline the curve of her chin.

The door opened, making the house shudder. His uncle stood against the daylight so all the boy could see was his silhouette. A hunting knife in one hand, he stepped into the house with such heaviness, Lukas could feel the vibration in the wall of the cabin against his back.

—Where have you been?

—To town.

—Why?

—To see the shopkeeper.

—What for?

—To see if there were letters.

The uncle came into the children's room now and saw on the bed the wrapping from the paper he'd bought at the store.

—What is that?

Lukas didn't answer, but the uncle began to understand. He went to the wooden Jesus in the corner and discovered there the money missing from his purse. He came back into the children's room and demanded that the boy turn over whatever he'd bought.

Lukas had slid the drawing of his mother into his sleeve. He'd hidden the paper in the sheets of his bed.

—You stole from me, said the uncle. Show me.

Lukas would not show him. He sat on the bed, fingering

the new pencil, and returned the uncle's stare.

The uncle slid the knife into a sheath on his belt. He gave the boy a look that meant, I will beat you if you don't do what I want, and I don't care what the beating will take out of me or you, I will have my way. His uncle had already welted the back of his thighs with a belt for disobedience. Having faced his punishments before, Lukas no longer feared his uncle. As he came at him, he leapt from the bed and ran around his legs toward the door.

For the second instance that morning, the boy was nabbed by the collar. This time, he screamed his sister's name.

When Ona heard her brother, she dropped her knife. What had Lukas done now? Two weeks ago, he'd been whipped for refusing to behead a chicken. Before that, he'd let a lamb wander into the woods while drawing the clouds. The boy dreamed too much—dreamed every wakeful minute, it seemed, just like their mother. Each time he was punished, Ona would gather the herbs to soothe his welts and plead with him to be good.

In the door of the house, she saw her uncle with a hand around her brother's neck.

—What's wrong?
—Go back outside.
—What did he do?

Now the paper in Lukas' sleeve fell to the floor. Seeing it, their uncle let the boy go and snatched up the drawing of the mother's eyes.

—Paper? You bought paper with my money?

He looked genuinely confused. He could not imagine wanting to spend money on something so impractical. Then his confusion gave way to anger.

—I feed you, house you, clothe you, and what do you do? Take my money without asking. What would your mother say? What would she do to you for stealing?

The boy struggled to get free. He expected his uncle to push him to the floor, take off his belt, and have at his backside. Instead, he grabbed a fistful of Lukas' hair.

He took the knife from his belt, pulled the boy's hair up straight, and cut. The blade wasn't sharp enough to slice through cleanly; he had to yank the locks up high and grind away, pulling his scalp so that Lukas yelped. When the first fistful fell to the floor, he howled with grief so acute that Ona, the obedient one, ran to her uncle to pull him away, but he knocked her down with a swing of his elbow and grabbed hold of the boy's bangs.

As the hair fell around him, Lukas's crumpled at the knees, hot tears filling his eyes. The uncle pulled and cut, pulled and cut, leaving bristle where his long brown locks had been.

Ona, on the floor, blood flowing from her nose, called out a hopeless protest and watched as her brother was transformed.

When their uncle was done, he let the boy go, sheathed his knife, and bent to gather the hair.

—I'll sell it to the shopkeeper to make up for what you took.

Lukas ran to his bed and hid himself under a quilt.

The uncle put the hair in a wooden bowl on the table and tossed the boy's drawing into the cold fireplace.

—Time to make dinner, Ona, he demanded, before walking outside to finish the butchering.

Once he'd gone, Ona rose slowly from the floor. She washed her face in a basin. She watched as blood dripped from her nose and diffused into the red water. Her brother was sobbing. What could she say? It would grow back, soon, but that didn't matter now.

She held a rag to her nose until the bleeding stopped, then went to the hearth to retrieve the drawing. She unfolded the page and looked at the face Lukas had rendered. Yes, it was their mother, he'd sketched her well, if roughly. Seeing her likeness, crumpled and begrimed with ashes, Ona feared she was dead. Ona had suffered nightmares of her mother's death but this was the first time the prospect crossed her waking mind.

Her uncle wanted dinner. Mother had said to listen, to obey.

She put the paper in her pocket. There would be a time to comfort Lukas, but now he was unreachable. She went outside to the cellar entrance and descended a ladder into the dirt-floored room. It always calmed her to be here alone in the dark, smelling the earth, the apples in the bin, the smoked sausages and bricks of cheese. Great chunks of ice from a nearby lake kept the room cold. On a wooden shelf, she and the uncle had placed spoils of past hunts. She took two chunks of rabbit, some potatoes and carrots and went back up to the surface, where daylight had faded and a moon shone over the pines.

The summer before last, in that stand of trees, she and her mother had gathered mushrooms together. Bending to the moss to cut free a chanterelle, Mamytė had said to Ona,

—Mushrooms grow everywhere, you can always count on finding them. One day we'll gather them across the ocean.

After she'd made a stew, she went into the room and lay beside her brother. He was pretending to sleep. She hugged him, whispered his name into his ear.
—Are you okay?
—I hate him.
She kissed his head as her mother would have done.
—It will grow back, she said.
He put his hands to his head, feeling his hair, astonished all over again by how little was left of it.
—I just wanted to draw Mamytė, he said.
She took the paper out of her pocket now and showed it to him.
—Why don't you finish?
—I can't draw her right.
—Of course, you can.
—I want her *back*, he said.
—We'll go soon, she promised.
—Let's go now, tonight.
—Don't be silly.
—We'll walk.

—We'd freeze.

—I like the cold. I never freeze.

She kissed him on his brow.

—Go to sleep, Lukas.

He snuggled closer to her and asked her to bring the atlas.

She rose and stood upon a stool in the corner of the room. She reached up high to a beam and pulled down the book Lukas wanted. Their mother had made it by hand, with leather and paper bought at great expense. It contained recipes for remedies she'd learned from her grandmothers and mother and intended to teach to her children in turn. Attached to the pages were envelopes in which she'd placed the dried herbs, roots, and powders that the recipes required. They called it an atlas, for she'd drawn by hand a map of the land all around the village, showing where you could find the trees, plants, and mushrooms needed to heal the ailments that so often afflicted the people then.

The recipes were in her handwriting, and beside them she'd inscribed advice they'd read many times in her absence.

For hurts that won't heal, drink broth of fresh alder leaves. Alder is the devil tree. Remember the story? God made the wolf fight the devil. The devil hid in the alder, but the wolf chased and bit his heel and blood poured down the trunk. Look for the red bark.

Have the priest bless your throat on Blaise Day, and drink the tea of these leaves for a healthy winter without me. I have blessed the leaves, and love your throats more than even God can know.

The herb of the Holy Ghost. In summer, it grows by the far fence. Angelica root hung round the neck dispels sorrow.

—Can I have some caraway seeds? Lukas asked in the dark.

Ona turned to the page and looked into the little envelope.

—There's plenty left, she said.

Lukas liked to chew on the seeds. The mother had told him that when he was a baby and tormented by evil dreams, she'd placed a dish of boiling water and caraway seeds beneath his cradle. The fragrant steam had calmed him, the dreams had ceased, and so she'd always kept a bowl of the seeds on hand.

His sister gave him a pinch of the seeds, and he slipped them into his mouth and began to envision the distance between himself and the shores of America. Europe he could grasp—the distance between the village and the port of Hamburg, on the map in the basement of the church, was as long as his ten-year-old hand. But he hadn't seen a map of the ocean—the page came to an end with England. His sister said it wasn't so wide, the Atlantic. She'd seen a globe once, when a teacher visited from Kaunas, and the ocean looked no bigger than a loaf of their mother's bread, which was no wider than the boy's chest. And so, he shut his eyes and pictured a tiny boat, the size of a caraway seed crossing the hill of his ribs, over his heart, onward to the far shore.

II

Marija curled and shivered in the damp sheet. It was still dark, but Karolina could see the sweat beading her nose. She'd worsened overnight, had been sick for five days—the grippe—and her breathing was shallow.

They were cousins, these women. Six months earlier, Karolina had joined Marija in his tenement. Their room, they hoped, was temporary. It felt unreal, like some dreamed up box, a grey purgatory. It contained two small beds, a heavy oak wardrobe they shared, and a trunk.

Karolina went to the window and looked into the predawn dark. She liked sometimes to stand here and watch the light come in. Already the sky over the tenement across the way glowed faintly purple and blue.

Below on the street, hidden by darkness, a horse pulled a cart over cobbles. The crunch of the wood wheels pleased her. That unseen animal was like God, she thought—known by its soft, secret sound. She tried to pray for her cousin—*don't let her be next*—but the horse had vanished around a corner and could be heard no more.

The grippe had already taken one soul on this floor, a baby born only three months ago. Once ill, he hadn't survived a week. The mother had had it, too, but recovered to bury him; she had not spoken a word to anyone since and ate almost nothing; her weeping could sometimes be heard through the walls at night.

Now Marija. Today she would need more tea—chamomile flowers much like those Karolina had brought from the homeland wrapped in a handkerchief. They'd run out after a bout of autumn illness, and Karolina had been lucky to find more in a nearby market. Just a day ago, she'd used the last of the replenishments in the pot Marija drank before collapsing into unshakeable sleep. She was slumbering still, her eyes scarcely open, glassy with feverish dreaming.

Karolina watched the sky over the tenement begin to swell with delicate light. She thought of home, snow heaped outside the door, ice on the eaves, her two children in their beds sleeping. She thought to pray for them, but was distracted by the snoring of her Polish neighbor—a ragged rumble like the growl of saws at the piano factory where she worked. Someone—maybe their elder son—was pushing wood into the kitchen stove. She could hear the squeak of the stove door, the knock of kindling falling inside that iron belly, and rats in the walls. She'd had nightmares about them. The rodents spoke a nasty fast English, told her to get out, this room belonged to them. She knew it. In her dream last night, she promised the rats she'd go back on the first boat, just as soon as Marija was well.

But Marija was not well, not even close. She had never been strong. She was too thin. Karolina could see the curve of her cheekbones, the sharp rise of her clavicle under her throat. Every day the grippe killed big strong men; it could kill Marija with ease.

Karolina whispered the words of the Hail Mary, but as she did, she thought of all she must do that day. She would buy the chamomile, find a doctor, and, if it could be had, elderberry syrup. And more honey. Along the way, she would have to stop at the factory to beg for more time off from work to care for her cousin.

Outside, the dawn's glow diffused upward, over all the street, and she could see below the sheen of the stones; cold rain had fallen overnight, or had it been snow? Frost laced the pane. From out of the tenement opposite, two dark figures emerged—boys with caps and wool jackets. They paused after coming into the street, looked this way and that as if deciding which way to go: their first decision of the day. Turn left and one fate awaited them; turn right, another. Either way, their lives would be forever changed. The city played tricks in all directions. What awaited them? A pickpocket? A benefactress? A new job in a stable or scrubbing floors, or a reckless hansom to knock them down in the mud? Everywhere you looked, people casually made irreversible choices. The boys went left. Karolina's heart went out to them. They had no idea, really, if left was the right way for them. How could they know? From up here, on the fourth floor, their lives looked dreadfully chancy.

They were small creatures but looked like they knew where they were going. Karolina rarely felt so sure here in New York. Often when walking about, pulled into the flow by some urgent errand to buy food or go to her work—some duty that could scarcely be avoided or delayed—when thus directed toward some definite destination, Karolina would be visited by the keen temptation to stray from her assigned purpose; the sight of some dark, unexplored street or alley would beckon her, and she would stop, stare, and consider the prospect of walking right out of her own small life into another. She had never before experienced this urge to wander; it was the city that produced such effects, for it was filled with strangers whose existences were always arousing her curiosity and desire. What to make of the Italian fruit seller now setting himself up for business on the street corner below? He was there every morning, as reliable as a clock, with his shiny bald head topped with its cap, a mole on his cheek, a long severe frown on his face, and only four fingers on his left hand. And here was the old lady in the window opposite, rising from her bed with great slowness, as if she were half in her grave, in a room that Karolina would never have cause to enter. What treasures were kept there? What hidden secrets in drawers, what scents in what bottles from what countries the world over?

The boys had disappeared. How had they known left and not right? She often wondered, home or here? Stay or leave? Work or quit? But she had no real choices. She just liked to pretend she did. Sometimes the pretending seemed to matter more than anything else.

A kettle was whistling in the kitchen. One of the Poles with whom she and Marija shared these rooms was making tea. Would they lend her chamomile if they had it? She doubted it. They were unfriendly to Karolina. They scarcely talked to her. Anyway, she relished the opportunity to leave the building and find her own tea. Three days she'd been cooped up with Marija. Three days absent from work—by now, she'd probably lost her place. She'd told the man at the factory, also a Pole, about her sick cousin. He'd pretended to not understand. A cousin? What cousin? Work went on regardless of cousins, not to mention children and husbands and wives. Still, she'd insisted: *I can't work tomorrow*. He'd shrugged. They'd stood face to face in the din of the factory, the hammering and sawing and sanding. What had the shrug meant? She didn't know, but she'd lose the job if necessary. A job could be replaced; a cousin could not.

She looked at Marija. Yes, worse. Pale and hot, her face looked unreachable, buried in sleep. As children, they'd played in the Merkys, practiced kissing under a bridge, ridden horses bareback in fields. The sister she'd never had, the girl with answers, who knew the ways of the world before other children. She would live. Karolina would find tea; she would bring back a good doctor, someone to help. The Polish mother might know; there would be a doctor nearby, in one of these gray buildings, hidden inside a dim room, waiting to be summoned. Would he understand her? What language would he speak? Polish, Yiddish, or Russian?

She knew a market on Broadway where she could at least find the chamomile flowers—a distance of some twenty blocks from this corner. A Lithuanian man worked there. A small man with hair in his ears, he sold all manner of herbs from his cart in the Gansevoort market. He would have the *ramunelė* that smelled not unlike the flowers that grew so thickly along the Merkys, attracting bees whose hum you could hear ten meters off on warm summer days. He'd have honey, too, in round gold jars. She would buy some for Marija and maybe, if she could find them, lemons.

First, she had to bathe. In the washroom, she filled a metal basin with water that was lukewarm, cloudy, flecked with minerals. Bracing for the shock, she tore off her nightdress and stepped into the bath. A sharp chill ran up her body. She moved quickly with a rag and piece of soap, washed herself with loud splashes and gasps. When she could stand it no longer, she hopped out like a bird and with frantic motions dried off with a rough towel.

Back in her room, she yearned to sink back into the bed, to cover herself with blankets that still smelled of home. Instead, she pulled her clothes from the wardrobe—a dove-gray dress with black buttons, gloves of black leather, hand-stitched in Krakow (inherited from her once rich grandmother), tall boots and stockings and a hat of black fur. The warmth of the fabrics made her feel better at once. She smelled winter in the wool of her coat. She could hear voices from the street below, the laugh of an old woman rang out, the jangle of a harness, wheels rattling over stones, and pigeons thrumming with hunger over rubbish in gutters.

She looked forward to talking with the man in the market again. They'd met three times before. In their first meeting, they learned they were from the same region, knew the same lakes and towns, and even had a distant cousin in common. He would be able to give her what she needed. It wouldn't be hard to get there. Shorter than the distance from home to church, which took almost two hours on foot. Three with snow on the ground, as now there would be. Snow all around the house where her children slept.

She went through the kitchen, to the door that hid the Polish family's room. Each day, the two older boys went to a nearby school, the husband left at dawn to work, and the woman stayed behind with a smaller boy, sewing. It was her baby who'd died from the grippe two weeks before. Karolina wondered if anyone would answer her knock.

It took three tries before someone did, a boy with a broad, circular face, pale as paper, looking up at her.

—Is your mother awake?

The boy turned, opened the door, called to his mother, who was sitting in a chair by the fire, already sewing her piecework. An older boy was in the act of pushing his pale leg into trousers.

Slowly, the woman, wearing a mourning dress, came to the door, presenting her thin, dour face to Karolina, who asked in Polish for a doctor who could help Marija. The woman replied that doctors here were no good, they could do nothing but watch. It was better to forget them and pray.

—Please, said Karolina. My cousin could die.

The woman went back into her room and took something from the mantel. She returned with a doctor's visiting card. It was white with black type that read Pietr Sadowski, Medical Doctor, and gave his address on MacDougal Street.

The woman's face looked worn from grief. She regarded her neighbor skeptically. When you'd lost a child and seen it swallowed by a hole in the ground, when your offspring could come and go so lightly from the face of the earth, were any people ever completely real again? Did they all look prone to disappearance? Karolina felt accused, but what had she done but assert her presence, her need, her faith in doctors?

She thanked the woman and returned to her room to check on Marija. Her cousin had shifted position, curled her body more tightly, hidden her face in the damp sheet. Karolina rubbed the curve of her hip through the quilt. She whispered her name, then spoke it aloud, but Marija did not move. So, Karolina put her hands on her face. Her cheeks were blazing hot, her lips chapped; she needed water. The teacup on the floor by the bed was half full with cold tea, the last of it. Karolina held this up to Marija's mouth, exhorting her, lifting her head up to the cup, and at last her eyes fluttered open. She sipped, then fell back to the pillow, bewildered, her eyes roving.

—I'm going out, Karolina whispered. To find a doctor and more chamomile for you.

Marija's eyes fluttered shut, her head lolled sideways

and back, so her chin pointed up to the ceiling. Her breathing came heavy, rough, shallow. Had she heard? Had she understood? Either way, she would sleep now, there was no reaching her; her mind was far off. Karolina rose to her feet slowly, taking one last look at Marija's slender face, noting its pale complexion, and the deep hollows under her eyes.

She walked out, her step quickening as she went down the hall, hoping to hear Marija call out her name, but no sound came. She reached the door and abruptly entered the stairwell—a dark chasm at the core of the building, many stories winding. The well had its own smells—of cooked potatoes and garlic, of bodies aging, of dog and rat. Now, unusually, the perfume of someone who'd happened to descend not long before. Karolina was turning the scent over in her mouth, trying to place it—for the smell seemed to hint at a familiar fantasy—when she pushed the door open and stepped outside.

Did anyone notice her entrance upon the stage of the city street? It seemed at least that one soul did. He stood on the corner of Henry and Clinton with a newspaper under his arm, pigeons waddling near his shiny black boots. He looked at her face with concern the moment she appeared outside, just as if he'd been waiting for her to arrive.

He watched as she pulled her coat tightly around her waist. She noticed his dark coat, his mustache and black hat, the pocket watch he fingered in his left hand. She turned away from his gaze and walked.

A ceiling of cloud made Manhattan seem a cellar. So many creatures prowled about inside it, upon its wet floors. She joined them, one foot after the other. A horse-drawn cart crammed with coal split the street in two with a racket. A snow flurry began.

—Lemons, lemons, lemons!

A cart full of melons went by. A confused Slav pushed it over stones, calling out in a weary voice. His wares were melons, not lemons—Karolina had learned as much shopping in the Gansevoort market – but no one on that street cared to correct the error.

Meanwhile, the man in black was following Karolina, she sensed, at a distance of some twenty paces.

—Lemons, lemons, lemons!

She smelled the melons. Their pungency blended pleasingly with the stairwell perfume. The scents were closely related—each a village cousin to the other.

Her husband had been such a cousin. A distant cousin

with the same complexion as hers. Not long ago, he'd stood naked without shame on a riverbank, perfectly formed, smiling down at her. A poor relation, gruff and careless, but so, so handsome, a man with a quick smile and able hands. He'd wooed her, she'd been glad to let him. In a city, scents could connect in the same way, with erotic charge, and then vanish just as quickly as her husband had. Tomorrow the scent of melons would be elsewhere; the perfume would drift away; never again would the scents cross.

—Lemons, lemons, lemons—

The voice faded. She heard the rattle of the cart on the stones behind her. She was gliding now onto Clinton Street. The man in black followed.

III

On Sunday, Lukas and Ona walked to church. They stopped in the village to watch the Cossacks' horses playing in the pasture. The red mare raced to the fence, turned and galloped to the other side. Powder glittered in puffs behind her.

A boy appeared in the stable doorway holding a shovel. Dust and dung clung to his boots and leggings, and his long black bangs were slick with sweat. He stared at Ona and Lukas as they passed.

The church bell pealed the air clean. Mass began with an old hymn. The liturgy would be in Latin, the singing in Lithuanian. Thirteen men, women, and children stood stiffly in coats as the small priest from Varėna cried out the gospel, his breath pluming the air.

Most of their relatives had left the country to escape conscription, or because they'd had no land, or had sought adventure abroad. Those who remained raised their voices, but the quiet between hymns descended like a judgment upon the smallness of their lives.

Even Karolina had left, and without her daughter and son. The villagers missed her soprano voice at mass. They missed her advice in the ways of healing and charms culled from the woods. She had been the only educated woman they'd known, the child of an unusual marriage—her mother a Lithuanian beauty, her father a Pole and heir to a lost estate. Now dead, he'd somehow managed, with what remained of his inheritance, to send her to school, and so Karolina knew more of the world than most.

What would become of her children, the people wondered? The boy Lukas had a wild look about him—dirty clothes, a wariness about the eyes, and now his hair, once long and tangled, was cut roughly down to the scalp. Embarrassed, he'd been slow to take off his cap. And the girl—skittish as a deer, shrouded in impenetrable silence, suffering the crucible of adolescence alone, without another woman in the house. Their mother had been landless, abandoned by her husband, and dependent on an unkind in-law. She had reasons for leaving—but without her children? Some thought it inexcusable, no matter how sharp the hunger that drove her to it. Others thought it an act of courage to trust her fate to the distant storm of American wealth.

The children knelt in the back row. They trained their eyes on the shopkeeper, who would or would not have the letter from their mother in his pocket. They went to church every Sunday because their mother had told them they must. She had raised them to believe in angels, in the goodness of Mary, the miracles of Jesus. She'd taught them, too, that trees had spirits, as did bees and streams and serpents. She'd never learned to doubt myth and legend. She could take in the conjectures of any priest or mystic and make room for them in her heart. For Karolina, belief was as common and inevitable as the moss and fungus of the forest.

And so, her children knew what it was to pray. They prayed not to Jesus, but to some larger spirit that took part in the motion of planets only their mother could point out in the night sky.

The priest was consecrating the bread. It had been made by the shopkeeper's wife, a rough loaf of rye grown and milled in the village. Knowing he'd sinned by stealing from his uncle, Lukas stayed behind as the others went to the altar to kneel.

Ona waited as the bald-headed priest made his way down the row, offering each mouth a morsel. She thought of the black-haired Cossack boy they'd seen on the way to church. She'd seen him only a few times, always from a distance, but she had the idea that he was playful and wicked but good, and she wanted to know him.

The priest's shadow fell over her. She took the bread into her mouth. The taste of rye and molasses mingled with the musty smell of the priest's old body.

When the mass ended, the priest exited out the side door, and the shopkeeper knelt on the stone floor of the church as the others shuffled out. The children waited for him, not daring to disturb his contemplation. They waited a long time, until Lukas' stomach rumbled with hunger and Ona went to the shopkeeper's side.

He was snoring softly, leaning like a stone against the pew. She whispered into his ear,

—Mr. Meizys, it's time.

He opened his eyes and saw the girl's face close to his. He smiled, showing his brown and broken teeth.

—I have something for you, he said.

He reached into his pocket and pulled out a brown envelope. On the front of it was the name of the village and the names of the children written in their mother's script. Lukas snatched the letter away and tore it open. A strange green paper fluttered to the floor—money, it was a bill—no, two, and each marked with a twenty in the corner. They'd been folded into the letter itself, which had been written on butcher's paper.

The old man and the children read together in the empty church.

My children—

I've written to Father Rambauskas to ask him for help. I haven't enough money for your passage, but here is some, and he will have more, and maybe your uncle, too. I am sorry to still have so little. It is expensive here, but I am too sick from missing you. Ask Rambauskas for help. You can count on it. He is a good man. When you have enough, you have my blessing to travel to Hamburg by train.

I send you my love, children. Be good, stay healthy, and have faith in your mother and God.

Mamytė.

—She wants us to come? said Lukas, still looking at the words.

—Doesn't she know Rambauskas was exiled? asked the shopkeeper. And how foolish to think he would have money for you!

Her heart thrumming, Ona took the letter from her brother and reread it. Had her mother meant it about their coming? What did it mean that she was *too sick* from missing them? The girl was frightened. Before her brother could see her cry, she dropped the letter, and ran out of the church. Lukas picked up the paper and money, folded them into his pocket and chased after her.

The shopkeeper dropped to his knees, put his blue hands together and resumed his praying in the cold.

Ona dashed through the churchyard and didn't stop running until she'd reached the edge of the village. Lukas caught up to her there.

—She wants us to *come*, he cried.

—We don't have enough.

—We'll get the rest from Uncle.

—Are you joking?

—Then we'll *steal* it, he said.

—He has nothing to steal! Not enough, at least.

—But we have to go. I hate him!

Ona frowned and looked across the river, where the red mare stood in the pasture. As if she could feel the girl's gaze, the beast turned to look back at her. For a long time, horse and child stared at each other across the half-frozen water.

—Maybe, whispered Ona.

—Maybe what?

—Maybe there's another way.

Their uncle hadn't attended church in years. He had faith in his own bodily satisfactions and not much else. Sunday deserved nothing out of the ordinary so he made a meal of leftover stew and drank homemade schnapps. He was almost drunk when the children returned. Their faces were so red and young he couldn't help but be pleased by them. When Lukas took off his cap, he felt a pang of guilt for the punishment he'd exacted. He offered them what little was left of the stew the girl had made the night before, and they ate it quickly. He'd promised his sister-in-law they would always have three meals a day—the one promise he'd made, and one he could keep.

He pestered the children for news from the village.

When Ona told him about their mother's letter, he frowned and said,

—You should stay here. Who knows what America is?

The children looked pathetic. What could he do with such creatures? They were his sister-in-law's kids through and through—moody, distant, mischievous, spoiled. They lied to him daily; they resented his odors, his ugliness.

—Did she send any money?

Neither child wanted to reveal the truth for they feared their uncle would take the money and hide it away. They hesitated in answering and looked at each other instinctively, so that it became clear to their uncle that the answer to his question was yes.

—Show it to me, he said.

The boy slowly took the bills from his pocket. He placed them on the table. All three of them inspected them, the first dollars they'd ever seen.

In the center of each bill, a rich-looking, handsome man, was bound in an ornate oval. The number twenty appeared in a flowering pool of ink. Twenty dollars: more than cash, a sign of providence, of lavish rooms built for tycoons. Most of the words on the bills they did not know, but they unfurled with such graphic richness that they grasped their deeper meaning. The understanding was a bitterness, for it meant they had only a piece of the whole, and the whole was boundless and golden and impossibly far away.

—How much was her ticket? asked their uncle.
—About a hundred-and-fifty German marks.
—What of dollars?
No one knew.
—I'll go to the village in the morning, he said. I'll talk to the shopkeeper. He'll have an idea.

The children watched their uncle carefully. For the first time, they needed his confidence, his experience and understanding of life. But his face was dark. He drank his schnapps and stood from the table and said he needed to rest.

They listened to the creak of his bed and the heavy sigh. Lukas leaned over the table and whispered,
—Can you draw a map?

She took his pencil and a sheet of the paper the boy had bought. She began to sketch the boundary of the Baltic Sea.

They sat at the table, burning the candles down so that they might chart from memory an outline of distances they could only imagine.

Ona had also seen the map of Europe in the basement of the church. She'd studied it carefully for a geography test administered by the priest in the secret school, before the Russians shut it down. She'd been able once to locate Danzig on a map, and Dusseldorf, and Riga. But that was a year ago, and now her hand wavered as she drew a border between the Russian and Prussian empires.

—We are somewhere here. Here is Poland, here the shore. Prussia, Germany, and Hamburg here, further west.

—Far?

—Very.

—Did anyone ever walk so far?

—Napoleon's army went further.

A stiff wind pressed against the house. They looked from the drawing to the black windowpane that hid the night. They had never ventured further than the town to the west where their mother had bartered mushrooms for books. There lived a man, a friend of their mother's, a smuggler of books. He had connections in Poland. He'd given the children chocolate from Krakow.

—Do you remember the man in Varėna? said Ona.

—With the bushy eyebrows?

—He could help us.

—I think he would, said the boy, remembering the chocolates. So, what do we do then? Go to him?

The boy looked to his older sister, expecting her to have an answer; he had unreasonable faith in her capacities. She knew this and loved him for it, but she didn't know how to respond.

—Mother would tell us to sleep, she said. Maybe we'll dream an answer.

Soon Ona was resting beside her brother, thinking of the horse they'd seen in the village.

She imagined the dirt road scarcely visible in the snow, snaking from Varėna to Zervynos. A bridge over the frozen Ula. From the Ula to Marcinkonys. From Marcinkonys to Druskininkai, to where? Vast stretches of forest and fields, the villages of Suvalkija and Prussia, until they came to the city of Danzig on the sea. By horse, how many days? By foot, how many months?

Why had their mercurial mother written such a tormenting letter to them in the depths of winter, when roads were difficult and they'd no money at hand? She'd written that she wanted them to come now if they could— not later, but now.

She'd left from Varėna by train. That day they'd waited

for hours at the station without complaint. Their mother had her one bag. She had her ticket. She wore on her lapel some violets the children had picked for good luck. It'd been a clear April day, bright skies taut with dread as the tracks trembled, signaling the train's approach.

The black steel engine made a monstrous noise. It filled up the world, left no space for all the children had known and loved—their mother's soft hands, her tall beauty. In the shadow of the train, she looked small and afraid. But then she smiled and kissed their heads, tears in her eyes, promising to send for them soon.

Ona sat up in bed and lit a candle on the floor. She opened their mother's book of remedies and read the recipes to help her fall asleep. But her heart was pounding, and then her brother began to talk in his sleep.

He declared in the dark:

—The storks!

A summer dream of storks, the great traveling birds of their homeland. A sign, their mother would say.

IV

Henry, Grand, Broome, Orchard, Pearl—she'd learn the words if she lived here long enough. *Clinton* would come to mean melons and dung puddles, vendor cries and men in alleys. One such man came now—rat-faced, craven, rail thin, he surfaced from an alley and whistled. She side-stepped him and a puddle at once. The flurry quickened. The sky blushed a darker purple.

Her boots would not last the winter. A hole in the sole was growing. Snow would soon soak her stockings. What price to cobble a boot? It would have to wait; she hadn't much money after sending her savings to the children, and some of what she had now would have to go for chamomile, honey, and the doctor's fee. On the way, she would stop by the piano factory to beg for more time off. Perhaps, if her boss was feeling charitable, he'd advance her a dollar's pay.

On the corner of Henry and Clinton, she tried to remember with exactness how her children looked—the girl's long angular face, narrow, knowing eyes of green, and the boy's jocular smile, his freckled cheeks pillowed with fat. How dare she leave them? But she had—entrusted them to her husband's brother, who'd do the minimum and think it a sacrifice. His farm was the only home the children had known. She'd given birth to them there, under her brother-in-law's roof, for her husband had never had his own land and neither had she. The only way she could see to escape the uncle's charity was to emigrate alone.

A policeman on a horse clopped by. The horse shat with a twitch of his heavy brown tail. He looked like a Cossack, this officer—the same haughty posture, the same dark hair and mustache. Karolina had the feeling she was being watched and turned around to see where she'd been. The sidewalk was empty. She noticed a shop selling maps, the world displayed in its window. She walked back to look more closely.

The continents were green and messily spread over the face of the earth. How disorganized of God to place oceans between one land and another. Her homeland was subsumed by the empire to the east. In the heart of Manhattan, one could be excused for not believing in its existence.

In the glass, her reflection blended with a reflection of a black horse stomping on the stones behind her. On the other side of the window a black hat floated by, and a pair of hands removed its gloves. Black and supple, they glistened, as so much in this country did—men's canes and boots, the cobblestones and carriage wheels. Even the gutters sparkled. She tried to see the man to whom the gloves and hat belonged, but whomever it had been receded into the velvet darkness of the shop's interior.

She turned to face the black horse. Its head loomed nearby, its wintry breath fogging the air. She glimpsed a reflection of her face in the beast's eye and recalled a Cossack riding his horse through the village; he'd looked down at her and winked. Often while she was walking this city, memories of home swelled up in her this way and left her bereft. She knew there was no time for such moodiness. There was too much work to be done—barrels built, merchandise bought and sold. Sewing machines could be heard from windows above. A man bolted through a saloon's doors, charged up Clinton faster than her thoughts could move.

She pressed on through the squalid street, and all around her life teemed and hurried. Here trotted a speckled swine, past a gang of urchins rolling dice beneath a balcony festooned with laundry—a red dress, knickers, dingy gray drawers. There, a fat woman called down to the boys in what language? This block was more Jewish than not, it must have been Yiddish. Every corner you turn, new voices and faces, but always the same needs—shelter, food, clothing, water, heat. The ash pits and garbage, the stockpiles of wood and coal, fruit carts and butcher shops. The swine knocked over a pail of trash with its snout. Potato peelings, blue with rot, spilled onto the street, reeking. Karolina shied away, tried to round the kids with their dice from behind without success. She tripped over a boy's foot and fell.

Jeers and curses erupted around her as she crashed into the middle of their game. She rested a moment, dazed. She felt seasick as if the island were a boat in the waves. She got to her knees, looked down at the dice, at the boys' faces—curious, freckled, confused. They looked back at her. One of them said something to the others, and at once they scooped up the coins and dice on the ground, then sauntered away.

She knelt on her haunches and breathed deeply, but the stink of garbage made her head spin. She retched weakly as men in boots strode around her, one obstacle among many. She felt in her coat pocket for a handkerchief. All she found there was the doctor's visiting card. She looked at it as sweat cooled her face and neck.

What was coming over her? Perhaps she ought to give up this quest, return to the flat, but the air in the tenement was worse than the street. Here at least she could see the sky. It was only a matter of will. One foot after another. Slowly, she began to rise.

She saw them now, the same group of boys, gathered in a clump half a block away. One boy pushed another, who came back with a swing of his fist. From both assailants now the punches came wild and free; the little elastic arms were a blur, their tiny fists landing with soft thuds. Rivulets of blood spilled from pale noses. The weaker boy, smaller but more ferocious, fought like a rabid thing. He had long brown hair like Lukas, a fair face with enormous eyes. A solid hit to his jaw sent him sprawling to the pavement. The bigger child straddled him and lifted his arm to strike.

Karolina had pushed her way through the throng. She

grabbed hold of the boy's elbow, yanked it back, pulled him off his opponent with a burst of violence. She knelt to the small boy's side, speaking in Polish: This must stop, look at your face! She helped him to his feet, and the blood flowed from his nose as he stared at her with fright and defiance. The boys around him were laughing, mocking him. She snapped at them all so fervently that their mouths shut at once. Did they think her a witch? Had she cursed their lice-bitten heads? She glowered and pulled the boy away from them, toward a saloon she'd passed. Her errands could wait.

The crowd parted, let them through. The boy didn't resist as she pulled him away by his upper arm. She kept talking in Polish, suspecting he could not understand her, hoping he would:

—You look like my son. You fight like him, too. That could get you killed someday if you're not careful. Stay away from those idiots!

He said something back to her. English. Too many languages in the air, too many nouns to know. He said the same words again, and she caught hold of one: *eat.*

Eat, water, love, island, city, onion, mushroom, potato—these and other odd nouns she had gathered. They would not get her far in Manhattan, but here, where so many spent so much of each day hungry, *eat* was a word one quickly learned.

Inside the dark saloon, men wrapped in coats sat in cold stupors. An aproned man stood tall behind a wood counter, guarding bottles of liquor. She spoke to him in a mix of Polish and Russian, telling him to bring a wet rag. He understood nothing, blinked at her, then the boy.

A drunk swerved out of the dark with a grin and spoke to her in indecipherable English. The barman muttered a few slippery words back. An argument erupted. Karolina, tightening her grip on the boy, pointed to his face and shouted in Russian:

—Rag, please?

Somehow understanding, the barman produced a glass of water and tossed her a cloth. She used these to wipe the boy's mouth, cheeks, nose, and neck with a rough, determined hand. He scowled as she did it, shrinking from her touch and the cold wet rag.

As she tended to him, she thought of Marija, suffering alone. It was wrong to delay her errands, but here was a boy who needed to eat, who looked so much like her own son. She turned to the barman, hoping he'd be kind.

—Food? she said, in English, pointing to the child.

The man pointed to a table, and Karolina sat down at it with the boy to wait. He looked at her shyly as she asked him where he was from in badly broken English. He said nothing in reply. His mouth was very small, very closed and tight, as if he were hiding something inside it that wanted to get out. His green eyes were just about bursting with secrets, the way they sparkled. Had it been the first time he'd been beaten by that boy, she wanted to ask? Was it hard being out in the street with the roughs? He wasn't one of them, she could see that. He was tender, prideful but weak.

The soup came, a clay bowl of steaming potato chowder. He dug in at once, and she watched him spoon it in in nice big bites, not looking up until he was half done. She saw the soup pass in slow gulps down his throat. His dark, greasy hair kinked up near the crown. His hands looked small and delicate, the knuckles on his left hand bright with blood. There were no other hands that looked just this way. Countless children with scabby, rough-worn hands lived in this city, yet each one was dearly, potently singular. This boy gave off an air of melancholy. Children without their parents often did. Even her own, when spotted in their idleness, alone in a field under the immense sky, struck her as isolated, doomed, impossibly distant.

In her own language, she asked the boy where his mother might be. He didn't understand, but gave a wry smile and replied with some bright phrase that popped out of his mouth like a discovery. Well, bless you, she said, attempting to imitate the brightness of his voice, to reciprocate the indecipherable message, which he now amended with a longer utterance, a string of phrases that rattled off his tongue with such alacrity that she caught not one word. Still, in his eyes she read an intent, the urge to be known, recognized, by her, a stranger who'd taken the trouble to feed him. She reached out to touch his bloodied hand.

He pulled it away. His eyes hardened. He thought her strange; he'd become wary of her foreignness, which was a thick cloak she could not remove as long as she lived in this city. The boy with hair the same shade as her son's stepped away from the table, his eyes like cold dimes. She watched him go, sighed, and got up to leave herself.

But the barman called out to her, gesturing to the empty bowl. Ah, he wanted money! The anger in his face startled Karolina, who'd assumed, foolishly, the soup had been a small gift of mercy for a starving, brutalized boy in need of kindness. At least, she'd meant to ask for it in this spirit; she had no intention of buying a thing! But here was the barman holding out his big red hand.

She had no choice. Her coins flashed their dearness in the dark and disappeared into the barman's fist. Before leaving, she glanced at herself in the bar mirror. The cloudy reflection blurred her features; she seemed small, far-off, a specter. She turned away, feeling not entirely present in her own body.

In the street again, she closed her eyes to the daylight. When she opened them again, she saw a man in a black hat, black coat and gloves, idling on the corner, looking at a pocket watch as if it contained a secret known only to him. Was this the same man she'd seen before?

She turned, walked up the street into a crowd gathered round a cart selling some desirable thing she could not see for all the bodies bunched up to buy it—some food? A whiff of meaty steam moved past her. The thought of heavy food displeased her. No appetite, weakness of spirit, an inner cold—yes, she knew it now. The illness, the grippe, it would have her on the floor beside Marija soon. What then? Who would care for them? Who would help?

Somewhere nearby a church sounded the noon hour. The bells scattered pigeons, sparrows, awakened bums in beer halls. Those bells were so loud they might wake Marija, too. She looked up to find the steeple and saw nothing but black windows of tenements with brown facades. The last bell of the hour rang out, faded, as a gray nag pulled a load of ash down the street.

Pigeon shadows troubled her vision. She was out to buy chamomile, but when she rounded a tenement's corner and saw the tip of a steeple ahead, she moved toward it, thinking she needed to light a candle for Marija. Not to mention for herself, her children, and her dead parents. By June both their graves would be covered in weeds. There was no one to watch over them now. On the train to Germany, she'd promised to herself that she would not care anymore for such things as that. A proper American had no interest in graves. He only sought to stay out of his own as long as he could, by whatever means, and fatten his belly. The rats knew as much. There was one now, crawling out of a bin, alert and curious. With surprising dignity, its strong tail high in the air, the portly creature sauntered along the side of the building, found a gap in the brick wall, and ducked inside.

She came into the church's shadow, where three tramps sat side by side on wooden boxes, waiting, perhaps for blankets or bread from the priests. One of the men, shivering, his lips badly chapped and bleeding, called out to her for a coin. Never beg—that, too, had been a promise she'd made on the train.

She had to pull with all her weight to open the church door. Inside, she felt better at once. The cold, vaulted space, with its close scents and soft echoes, invited her further in, towards lit candles. They were arrayed before a baroque statue of Mary draped in blue, gazing vacantly into shadows. Karolina knelt and leaned her head in her arms. How pleasant to hear through the windows the soft clatter of horses outside, the city's ceaseless hustle made distant in this dim sanctuary. She wanted to sleep, to lie down on the slate floor. But she forced herself to her feet, took a stick from the sand, lit it, and touched the flame to the wick of a fresh candle.

She was not much for worship in the ordinary sense, but charms had their place. She'd had her babies baptized just in case and lit candles and fires on the right holidays. She respected ceremonial flame. It was right to trust the inscrutable powers; strong people always did. She'd learned that from her mother's parents, who could tell you when the earth felt right for planting. Her grandfather had the habit of feeling the soil. As a girl she'd seen him fondle the black earth, and sometimes even slip some into his mouth. He'd savor it with a look of abject hunger.

She tried to pray for him now, and for all her distant

kind, but a snore sounded from the pews. Prayer and oblivion shared the same space. Nothing stopping her from sleeping, too, but if she collapsed, she wouldn't rise before dark most likely, and then it would be too late to buy tea. She made the sign of the cross and left the Virgin in the dark quiet.

Outside, snow had begun to blow again. She turned around once, twice, reminding herself where she was and where she wished to walk. Meaning to go west, she took a step north.

V

The next day, the children followed their uncle into the village. Intending to sell Lukas' hair, he'd put it inside a linen sack their mother had once used to store her sewing things. Ona and Lukas would have refused to go on this wretched errand had their uncle not promised to ask the shopkeeper about the priest their mother believed could pay for their voyage to America.

But when they got to the shop, the old man shook his head at their uncle. There was no way to contact the exiled Rambauskas now. His money, if he had any, likely belonged to the Czar.

—What are we to do then? asked their uncle.

—Wait and hope she sends more money soon.

—It could be months. Years. The money might never come.
—Have faith, Kestas.

The uncle muttered, making an effort to prevent the children from hearing, but of course, they did:

—Their mother isn't dependable. She dreams too much. Just like my brother. He was a fool to marry her.

The shopkeeper shrugged. Their uncle sighed and opened his satchel. He took out two bottles of the homemade schnapps he'd brought to trade for molasses and flour. Then he removed the linen sack with the boy's hair.

Lukas ran out of the shop, slamming the door behind him—a futile protest. Ona hurried after him. When she caught up, she took his gloved hand in hers and squeezed.

—Let's go look at the horses, she said, hoping to cheer him.

—I want to leave now!

—We'll go. Soon. We just have to find a way, she said.

Not far off, in the stable door, the Cossack boy was grooming the mare. Ona walked toward him. He had a mole on his cheek and long black bangs and coal eyes. He stared at Ona, spat in the dirt, and asked what they wanted.

—Just to see the horses, she said in Russian.

—You can see them.

—Can we ride that one? she said, pointing to the mare.
—Don't be silly.
—Why is it silly to want to ride a beautiful horse?
He smiled. He clucked at the mare, brushed her neck, and cooed to her.
—Come, he said.
The children approached and reached to pet the horse.
—I can't let you ride her.
—Why not?
—My father would be upset.
—Where is he now?
—In the house next door.
—Is it hard living with officers?
—Why would it be hard? It's a good life.
—I never spoke to a Cossack before, said Ona.
—That's because you're a backward peasant.
—And you are a stable boy who shovels horseshit.
—Better than farming potatoes.
—Please let us ride her.
—You are ridiculous.
—Let us watch you ride her then, said Ona.
With languid motions he brushed the neck and withers. He laid a sheepskin over the back and placed the saddle on top of the wool. He removed the harness and put on

the bridle too roughly, so she jerked her head away. But he cooed and fed the horse a slice of apple, so that she settled down as he buckled the saddle and fixed the reins. With a boot in the stirrup, he pulled himself onto her back, and he and the beast pranced away into daylight.

The children followed and watched as the boy rode the mare in circles inside the fenced pasture. He looked tiny but skillful as he rode with ease.

He made the mare leap over a fallen tree. He made her trot and dance, then gallop hard at the children. He pulled to a fast stop before them.

—Could we ride her when your father is asleep? said Ona

—I said no.

—But you could arrange it. Tonight, under the moon.

Her daring silenced him for a moment.

—My father stays up late. The men drink and dance all hours.

Ona shrugged.

—Let's go, Lukas.

They walked back to the village store, but before going in, Ona turned to look at the boy. He was still watching her from atop the horse. He waved to her, and she waved back.

Inside the store, the uncle and the shopkeeper were

calculating how many German marks forty American dollars would buy. From the look on the uncle's face, the children knew they hadn't enough.

—They'll need at least twenty dollars more, he said.
—Then keep them with you, the shopkeeper said.
—They're *hers*, said their uncle.
—And she's gone, Kestas. It's your duty to take care of them.
—Old man, you don't need to lecture me. Bring me the flour. We have to get back.

They had to hurry because their uncle didn't want to return home in the dark. He wanted to be inside the house with the fire lit well before the sun swung low in the sky.

Night would come quickly. The sun in winter would not rise far above the pines. Clouds hid its shy arcing. In America perhaps winter suns would not be so shy. They would soar to the top of the heavens and hover there while the people below did their work.

They walked slowly, dawdling behind their uncle. An idea had surfaced in them—a fanciful idea, reckless, but tempting. It had the sheen of hope, the shape of a mare, and the color of blood. Lukas was the first to say it out loud.

—We could take the horse.

—I know, his sister whispered. At night, when the men are drinking.

—Just like our father, we could sell it for money and go.

Ona's face felt hot in the cold. It was wrong to steal. But she'd watched as the Czar's police had burned the school's books in the churchyard—books her mother had taught her to read—Bibles and hymn books, fairy tales and poems. One after another, they'd gone into the fire as the villagers were made to watch.

Now, walking behind their uncle, the children whispered their plans to each other. The future seemed to be hiding in the woods, almost visible behind every tree.

Would their uncle ever sleep? He fed yet another log into the stove and sat again in his chair to whittle away at a branch.

In winter, he carved figurines of Jesus sitting with his head resting on one hand. He sold them every March on St. Casmir's day in Varėna. It was nervous work for his hands as his mind raced. How many Jesuses for two tickets on the Hamburg Line? His fingers would fall off before he could carve so many.

The children had gone to bed. They kept their eyes open and listened. They heard his muttering now and then. They could see the glow of his candlelight beneath the door. Under the quilt they wore their wool stockings, their thickest socks and scarves around their necks. Ona had the atlas of their mother's remedies beside her. Lukas had stuffed two small satchels with food from the cellar—potatoes, apples, a round of farmer's cheese, a hunk of ham, a jar of honey.

The children snuggled under the quilt made long ago by their grandmother with the scraps of cloth given to her by a Russian soldier encamped near their village. In the patches they saw bits of rough army uniform, coarse to the touch. The quilt smelled like home, and they wanted to take it, but it was much too big.

Finally, they could hear their uncle's snoring.

They waited a few minutes more, then rose from the bed, and quietly put on their coats and boots, and hoisted their packs. Ona pushed open the bedroom door and saw their uncle in the chair, drool on his chin, a half-carved Jesus in his lap.

She went into the main room and crept to the figurine on the shelf in the corner. Hidden inside was the purse containing a small wad of rubles. Without counting, she stuffed the bills into her pocket, leaving the coins behind. Then she nodded at her brother, who stood waiting by their bedroom window.

He opened it. Dry cold gusted inside. She pushed him up and out, then followed with an agile leap.

They walked through the yard and stopped before entering the forest. They looked around at the snow-topped well, the frozen house silver in the moon and the expanse of snow swept over the pond where they'd once hooked carp. The hayfield glittered in answer to the stars.

The forest trail took them past the family graves. There on the hill above the marsh was buried one grandmother they remembered for having quilted the blankets, and another for the taste of her honey. They remembered their grandmothers' toothless gums, their age-spotted skin—these first lessons in decay. They had not known and never would know the other souls buried under the snow on that hill.

The moon climbed as they walked through snow that rose to the tops of their boots. Ona walked faster and often stopped to wait for her brother who struggled through drifts. Watching him, she began to doubt they would make it even to Varėna.

They frightened a fox on the trail. Its white tail flashed in the thicket. The moonlight was so lustrous the children could track the creature's progress through the woods.
—Do they have foxes in America? asked the boy.
—I'm sure of it.
—Not silver ones.
—Of course, all color foxes. Walk, Lukas. We don't have much time.

As they traipsed away from home for the last time in their lives, they began to fear they'd left something behind—some treasure they could never reclaim—though they did not dare turn back. They pressed on through the snow—Ona in front, Lukas struggling to keep up.

They could hear the Cossacks even before they'd reached the village. Muffled music—a fiddle, singing, dancing, clapping, the men's boots on the rectory floor. When the children came to the churchyard, they saw through the rectory window the shadows of men in the firelight.
—Come, whispered Ona, pulling Lukas toward the stables.
He hesitated. She looked at her brother and said,
—Maybe you don't want to go.

—I do.

—It's far.

—Napoleon's army went further—you said it yourself.

They walked on, crossing the square. As they expected, the stable door wasn't locked, and they closed it behind them. The smell of the horses was strong inside, but they could see nothing. They'd not expected to be so blind.

—Where's the tackle?

—To the right of me, I think.

They groped and tripped over each other. Lukas knocked over a metal bucket, it clanged against the wall. Ona opened the door to let in a bit of moonlight and now she saw the mare's solemn face staring right at her, surprisingly close.

Lukas opened the stall and led out the horse as Ona removed the tackle from a nail on the wall. Cooing as she'd heard the Cossack coo, she laid the sheepskin and saddle on the mare's back. When she tried to put on the bridle and bit, the horse bucked her head, bit at the air, nostrils flaring. Lukas removed an apple from his pocket. She took it at once, chomped it to pieces. He fed her another, and then she acquiesced, taking the bit in her enormous mouth.

The boy on one side, the girl on the other, they fastened the saddle and attached their packs to its belt loops. He whispered,

—I heard something.

They stopped to listen—the distant creak of a door.

She moved the bucket to the side of the horse, placed it upside down, then stood on its bottom, balancing. Hands on the saddle, she raised one foot into the stirrup and pushed herself up. With the girl on her back, the horse began to walk. Ona pulled the reins, and the mare reared, kicked Lukas in the shoulder and knocked him over.

A voice from outside called out.

—Who is it, who's there?

Lukas got up wincing and reached for his sister's hand. She pulled and he jumped, but he couldn't mount the horse. They heard the sound of footsteps—somebody running toward the stable. The horse loudly neighed.

—Get on the bucket!

Lukas did as she commanded, and his sister yanked him up with one hard pull. He swung his leg up and over and squeezed into the saddle behind her.

A man shouted from the yard. Ona let the horse bolt through the door. An officer stood just steps away from the barn, raising a pistol into the air. The mare ran right at him, so that he dived off into the snow, as they thundered on through the yard to the bridge.

They crossed it in two strides. The officer, on his knees, shot his gun, but he was too drunk to aim, and the bullet sailed over their heads.

It was fortunate for Ona and Lukas that he and his compatriots had consumed so much vodka that night. By the time they were sober enough to suit up and give chase, it was dawn; the children were well on their way to Varėna, and the snow was falling thick in the sky, covering all tracks.

VI

The great church shadowed her. Karolina shivered within herself and walked on with growing apprehension.

Had she left something behind in the pews? A prayer left unuttered? A candle unlit? There were so many saints and angels, so many faces of God in the world that her mind could not come to an end of prayer. To leave church was to leave the unsayable unsaid, the heart refreshed but yearning, and the mind more receptive to signs—signs of all sorts, and Manhattan supplied an abundance. They were coming at her now, a crowd of men in coats and caps, each body distinct, singular, briskly or slowly moving by. Their faces—they seemed to be signs, yes, but of what? What purpose swept them through these streets? What hungers, loves or ambitions? The harried, inscrutable faces moved too quickly past. But then she locked eyes on a particular face, one she had already seen—the long, knowing visage of a man dressed in black. He was fondling a pocket watch, looking at her—at *her*, as if his very purpose in being there, on the corner of that busy street, was to be in her sight.

She did not know him. Yet there he was, and there he had been, earlier in the day, when she'd walked out of her building, seen him looking at his watch just that way. He appeared to be a rich man. Maybe it was the clean lines of his coat, the polish of his boots, the cut of his hat. And his face—a bland, unreadable, pale, finely featured face, like that of the man on the twenty-dollar bills she'd mailed off weeks ago to her children. Yes, his face looked blessed with ease—unnatural ease on this frenetic New York day. She was afraid. She wanted to get away from him. She began to walk.

She soon came to the wide breach of Houston Street. Its airy expanse stretched to her left and right, the prospect in either direction intimating endless distance, block after powerful block heaped with buildings. She felt exhausted by the thought of traversing much more of this crowded island. When she saw an inviting knishery, she darted inside in hopes of losing her mysterious pursuer for good.

    She hadn't realized how noisy the streets had been, how cacophonous and riven with shouts, before entering this little oasis, this knishery, so hushed in comparison, for everyone here spoke at a lower volume—not softly exactly, but not loudly either. One ordered at a glass counter, where the wares were on display and a bearded man waited on customers who lined up patiently, mostly men but some women with children, too. There were many tables and chairs in the front and back rooms, where patrons sat with their coffee or tea and knishes. She was not very hungry but thought it would be good for her to have something warm to drink. She ordered a cup of tea and sat at a table in the front, with a view of the street.

    How good to sit! How tired she felt! She warmed her cold fingers on the hot cup before her. Just then, a mass of a man, appeared out of nothingness before her, speaking in polite Russian. He was asking her through his mustache if he might join her? There were no other free tables, it seemed. She nodded. He sat down with his knish and coffee. He was knish-shaped himself, balding, and had a kindly face. He sniffed a little, smiled, and thanked her before taking a first bite.

—How did you know I speak Russian? she asked him.
—Doesn't everyone here? And no harm in guessing. But you are not Russian, are you?
—No.

He raised his eyebrows, expecting her to tell him what she was.

Today was a day, though, when the answer was not entirely clear. She'd grown up in a stew of language: Lithuanian from her mother and grandmother; Polish from her father; Russian from teachers. She felt closest to her mother tongue, but it didn't help her in New York.

—I'm American, she said with a grim smile.

He laughed, flashing a gold tooth. She decided to like him.

—My home was a village two days southwest of Vilna, she explained. *Was?* She had never used the past tense in this way before. It troubled her.

—Ah, I have a cousin in Vilna.
—Where are you from?
—Minsk. We are neighbors.
—Yes.
—And here, too, we are neighbors. Even closer neighbors now. Children?
—They are back home.

—Ah.

—It couldn't be helped.

—Money will come. You are working?

She felt guilty now about buying a tea; every penny spent was not saved for them.

—My cousin is sick. I'm caring for her.

Her presence here, then, made no practical sense, she knew. She could hardly account for it without explaining the presence of the man with the pocket watch, but it was not entirely clear that he hadn't been a phantom, and she doubted this man from Minsk would understand.

—God bless her with good health, and you too, he said.

—You are kind to say so.

—We all need blessings. And elderberries. My mother would give me the syrup of elderberries when I was sick. It's hard to find here.

—My mother gave me that, too. So many berries were needed to make one drop.

—Elderberry syrup was my grandmother's magic. Until she died.

—I wonder if I could find some here for my cousin?

—In all of New York, there must be one vial of elderberry syrup, he said.

She looked down into her teacup, thinking of home.

The sweet, earthy elderberry scent of her memory became confused by the meaty smell of knishes and men. A swoon came upon her—a deep, inward, falling-down feeling that seemed to have no end, though she was sitting perfectly still. And though all four walls of the crowded knishery were stationary, the mirrors adorning them seemed to swirl, and she shut her eyes, leaned back, and held fast to the table. She dared not let go. The man was asking if she was alright.

—Just a bit dizzy, she said, as she opened her eyes and the room slowly righted itself.

—Perhaps you need some elderberries yourself, Miss.

—It's time I get on with my errands.

She rose from the table. The blood rushed from her head and shadows mobbed her vision. She paused to steady herself before saying goodbye to the kindly man from Minsk, who, before she parted, offered one last bit of advice,

—Take it slow—slow and easy! Keep an eye out for the horses!

Curious of him to tell her that, as if she were a child. The horses were everywhere, of course. Always a good idea to keep an eye out. Danger jostled, pranced, charged around each corner; horses knocked over drunks daily in the dust of these streets and scarcely anyone noticed. Keep an eye out—yes, of course, be alert. She exited the warm air of the knishery and stood again on cold gusty Houston.

There, again, waiting for her, with his pocket watch, the black hat and gloves, the man who'd followed her leaned on a lamppost across the street. No, she hadn't imagined him. There he was—she could see his pale face glance up from the watch, recognize her, and then glance away again, as if there were nothing at all unusual about his following her throughout Manhattan. A foul-smelling wind blew against her and him alike. It caught at their clothes as they stared at each other before a horse and cart came between them.

As the cart rumbled by, she began to walk west, as quickly as she could, on legs that seemed not quite hers; they spun beneath her with volition belonging to some fiercer, more determined creature than she felt herself to be. She held her head aloft in the cold, looking about with alarm, leery of horses, so many horses stampeding down Houston under the command of men who barked at anyone who came in their way. When she arrived at a cross street, she took it southward, away from the tumult of the thoroughfare.

The street was swarmed. On both sides, vendors sold their wares—bolts of fabric, undergarments, trousers, shoes, shoe leather. She spied a transaction underway, a woman buying white fabric, probably for curtains, a major purchase. Seeing money change hands made Karolina wonder if she had enough on hand for elderberry syrup were she to find some for sale. On Orchard Street, they sold nearly everything. Here, for instance, was a girl with long greasy blonde hair and a basket strapped to her body filled with tiny wooden tops for spinning.

—Tops? Tops? Tops for sale? she kept saying in English, in a wee voice, as the crowd jostled her along.

Blessed be the poor in spirit. The holy words came to Karolina now. She'd always doubted the notion, but this child made her wish it was true. She reached for her change purse. But then again, after the soup for the boy, after the tea in the knishery, she'd have to save her coins. Best to let this girl go on her way, calling out, now with a fierceness she'd failed at first to notice:

—Tops, tops! Tops for sale!

Karolina looked back at the way she'd come. The man with the pocket watch was nowhere to be seen. Of course, he was gone, attending to his own business. She'd been fearful of him, but now she wondered who he'd been, and why he'd singled her out, if in fact he had. Disappointment shadowed her, and confusion. She walked on, more slowly now, trying to remember his face, wondering again if he'd even been real.

Either the street widened or the crowd lessened, for the space around Karolina opened up; at last, she could move more freely about. Then, up ahead, like an apparition among a row of vendors selling cloth, strode a woman in mourning. She wore a dress of black lace and coat of black wool and a broad-brimmed hat with a fluttering veil. To protect herself from the snowfall, she held high a black umbrella with frilled edges. Arrayed in these woeful garments, the woman slowly made her way through the masses. Stricken with curiosity, Karolina watched as she walked down Orchard. For some reason, she didn't want to lose sight of this regal, richly-dressed woman. She followed a safe distance behind.

When the woman in mourning reached Delancey Street, she turned right, just as Karolina herself had planned to do. She walked neither fast nor slow but at a comfortable pace, so that Karolina did not have to rush or hold herself back to keep her distance. She was about twenty feet away and could see how she moved with a long, relaxed stride through the crowds, holding that umbrella high. It bobbed over all other heads, a beacon to follow, and when Karolina lost sight of the woman—for sometimes the crowds became too thick—she could still see the umbrella with the black silk fringe.

Karolina thought the woman must be mourning someone close to her—a husband most likely, for she looked very free in the way she walked. Perhaps she wasn't in the least bit sorrowful, but relieved—guilty for being so, but relieved all the same, now that she was on her own once again, and wealthy to boot, by the looks of her dress.... Which raised the question: What *was* this woman doing here on Delancey Street? What would call a rich, lonely widow down to these slums in the dead of winter?

The snow let up now, and sunlight came shimmering through. For some moments, the snow kept falling in the sun, like grace itself descending, and countless faces turned up to look. Karolina, too, paused to look at the light, and swooned in the street, touching her face. Yes, the fever—it was coming for her, too.

Hail Mary, full of grace, she muttered under her breath as she continued walking, reciting the rest in her mind, resolving to say an entire rosary by the time she returned home to Marija, if she could only keep her mind on it;

surely God would notice, would credit her a little for the effort?

The woman in mourning was still up ahead, some thirty feet away, gliding through the crowds, compelling Karolina to keep moving, too. She took a deep breath and resumed her journey.

VII

It was too dark to ride, but they had no choice. The mare bounded with dim sense down the trail. The forest came at them, a legion of trees; the wind tore at their ears. They could scarcely see the way as they moved through the bramble-choked waste of the marsh.

Lukas whimpered. He could feel the officer's pistol shot searing his skin, though in fact it had gone high into the night sky.

The mare slowed to a trot, to a walk, and a breeze swept the clouds away from the face of the moon. They came into a field resplendent with pale light. They rode across it on the mare, awed by their escape. Ona touched her brother's arm wrapped around her waist.

—Don't fall, she told him.

—I won't.
—Don't fall asleep either.
—I'm not tired, he lied.

They rode all night to get as far from the village as possible, and when the sky began to pale, they came upon a sleeping town. All its houses were dark and lined with a nimbus of snow.

The children knew so little of the world that even Varėna, with its modest cross-hatching of streets, seemed to them a daunting complexity. They feared becoming lost or discovered by an unfriendly stranger.

Their mother's friend Audrius, from whom she'd received books for the school, lived in this town. They'd been to his house three times before and intended now to ask for his help.

Audrius had been called many things in his life—a carpenter, a singer, an accordionist. Never had he been called a smuggler, though he was one. Those in that region who wished to read the word of God or man in their own language went to Audrius at night. He would travel to Prussia by horse to acquire the books. He hid them in secret compartments beneath his wagon, sewed them into the lining of his coat, buried them in barrels of grain, and so smuggled them home, where they might be read in private.

To reach his house, the children rode through town and turned down a dirt lane and followed it to the edge of the forest. There was his cabin and a barn behind it, shadowed by pines.

A small dog came running from the yard, yapping to greet the children as they clumsily dismounted. The door opened, and out came Audrius, a bulky man with shaggy gray curls and a knotted beard. He had the look of a warrior from an older time, a casualty of the Crusades.

After greeting the children, he asked where they were going.

—New York, Ona told him.

—Can your horse swim?

—We're going to sell her, Lukas announced, to pay for our passage.

Audrius looked doubtful, confused. Then he walked closer to the animal and inspected the brand burned into its flank. He looked darkly at the children.

—You look like death, he told them. Go inside and warm up. I'll take care of this horse.

As he led the mare to a small barn behind the house, the children went inside and waited in the hall. Through an open doorway, they saw his woodshop—a level, a hammer, and nails were strewn over a bench. On a table rested a coffin of pine, newly made.

The man returned and took the children into a kitchen warmed by a stove. They sat at the table as he prepared bread and butter and tea. It was a cave-like kitchen, the beams over the stove blackened with years of smoke. The walls seemed to have been soaked in garlic and onion juice. There were wooden crates of potatoes on the floor—easy pickings for mice—and a bowl of bruised apples on the table.

After he asked after their mother, they showed him her letter. He read it in a glance and handed it back.

—Of course, you want to go to her. But it's a long distance.

—We know.

—And that horse, he continued. I don't think you came by it honestly. If you did what I think you did, you're outlaws. The Russians will be hunting you. It's a matter of hours before they show up. What were you thinking? That you have wings?

The children were silenced. They looked at the table, their hearts beating quickly.

—What should we do? asked Ona.

—Let that horse go free and take one of mine.

They looked at him.

—I haven't much money, but I do have horses. You can repay me when you get to America, or not.

Then he produced a map—a page ripped from an atlas; the rough edge tore through Prussia. Roads, railways, and ferry routes marbled the paper; hundreds of names in tiny print floated over land and sea, all the names in Polish.

Audrius pointed to a spot on the map and traced a hair-thin dotted line meandering westward.

—This road—you see? You won't come across police here, at least not until you reach the border. It's badly kept. Hunters use it, trappers, mushroom gatherers.

He pushed the map toward Ona.

—Stick to the road, he said. Ask for help only when you need it. Sleep in churches. If you're polite, the priests should house and feed you.

Ona thanked him quietly. She felt cold in her bones as she traced with her finger the route to the border. It would be days before they reached it. Beside her, Lukas sat pale and scared. He stared into the map with eyes that seemed to see nothing.

Audrius dropped plates before them—sliced black bread smeared with butter. Then he poured them black tea and spooned gobs of honey into it. He watched them eat, smiling a little. They were their mother's children, truly, he said; she'd approve of their theft; she was that sort of spirit, the sort who did whatever it took. Good for them, he said, but now they'd have to be careful.

As soon as they'd finished their meal, Audrius said he'd walk them to the road. As they went through the house to the front door, Lukas paused at the workbench and put his hand on the smooth planks of the coffin. The wood was unfinished and fragrant, it glowed with a silky yellow light of its own.

—Who is it for? Lukas asked the room.

The man turned as he opened his front door.

—I don't know. Someone. There's always someone.

The coffin was cleanly made. It felt smooth to Lukas's fingers. He looked into its bright emptiness.

Ona waited for him at the door.

—What's wrong, Lukas?

—It's a long way, he said.

—Now we have a map, she replied. And a horse. Come.

Audrius gave them a colt the color of dark chocolate. Ona rode him warily at first, but soon recognized how well-trained he was, how responsive to her touch. At the slightest motion of the reins, or tap of her heels, he surged forward. He was thinner and lighter than the mare, and quicker on his feet.

The children walked the colt out of Varėna with Audrius limping alongside them. As they crossed a wide field covered in snow, he told the children what price they could expect to fetch for the colt when they tried to sell him across the border. Behind them the village was coming to life. They heard the squeak of an outhouse door, the slap of boots on a mat, the groan of a cow being milked.

They came to the forest and Audrius led them to a break in the trees.

—This trail leads to the road I pointed out on the map. Half a day west from the junction of the trail and road, you'll come to a monastery. The monks there often buy books from me. They're good people and will help. Do you understand?

Ona nodded.

The man wished them luck, slapped the colt and the children plunged forward into the woods.

They traveled into a stretch of land dense with pines that reared upwards from the earth, creating a canopy of snow-heavy boughs. The day came on clear, blue, and cold. The colt felt uneasy to Ona as they walked the trail. No markers guided them. Only footprints left by a traveler not long before helped them stay on course—if they did stay on course. Ona couldn't be sure. The wall of trees often broke in many directions, and multiple paths might be discerned at once, so that they had to choose to follow some sign, and the only sign were the prints in the snow. Ona could only hope they knew the way.

The silence menaced the children. The woods near their home possessed the same cottony hush—but because they were in strange country and could not recognize any trees, stones, or blueberry patches, the quiet in these woods felt sinister.

What they needed most was sleep. They'd been up all night. As the pale sun reached its low winter zenith, Lukas felt a quivering in his chest that he could not still. He seemed to hear the approach of Cossacks in the sound of every branch falling to the forest floor, in the caw of every blackbird.

He tightened his hold on his sister, who sat in front.
—What's wrong? she asked.
They had taken to speaking in whispers.
—I'm cold.
—Do you want to stop to eat?

—No.

He felt safer on the horse. With his feet on the ground, he could be more easily caught.

It was already past noon when the hunting trail led them to the road. The way was not much wider than the trail and not much more traveled either. Fresh wagon tracks stretched westward. They followed them.

In time, they heard voices. Soft voices, human, but male or female? How many? The sounds were distant but carried far. For an hour, the children and the colt followed the wagon tracks, listening to the voices.

The sun roved low; its pale face blinked through black trees; night would swoop down in hours. The children needed shelter and rest, but they wanted to remain invisible. They hung back and listened; the voices were too far away for them to understand.

The road turned and there at the end of it, the setting sun flared its last, washing them in cold light. Ona stopped the colt and shielded her eyes. She could see a clearing not far off. A field, after so much forest—it was like discovering a sea. A steeple topped by a cross rose above the tree-line.

VIII

A powerful gust flipped the black umbrella held aloft by the woman in mourning. She twisted and pulled at the contraption as the weather whipped up her dress hems. Soon she resumed her walk, moving swiftly along as if blown by the wind. At a slower pace, Karolina followed. Removing a glove, she touched her cheek; it blazed in the frigid air. A powerful shiver shook her as the woman in black disappeared into the crowd.

At the sound of a church bell tolling the half hour, Karolina was reminded of her purpose: chamomile, the doctor. And she had to report to her workplace to beg forgiveness for missing three straight days. Had she truly forgotten? Was she so out of her mind with illness? She might go back, take her place in bed beside Marija, but it was a long way home, and she wasn't so far gone that she could not place one foot in front of the other. She tunneled forward.

Even through the wind in her ears, she could hear the thudding of machines in the building beside her. Her factory, too, would be churning away at this hour, all the workers subsumed in labors, occupied with their strings and keys, their soundboards and timber, their odiferous varnishes.

She had been lucky to find a place in the factory. A young man in the tenement had told her of an opening there. He himself worked for the Weber factory as a tuner and told her one day, shortly after she'd arrived, that they needed a new hand in the key room. If she were quick, dependable, and very exacting, she could glue slats of ivory onto the ends of long wooden keys for a living. The very next morning, an hour before dawn, when the city was still dark and half sleeping, she walked the long way to Seventh Avenue with the young Pole at her side. He was terribly shy, a stutterer, and so walked in silence beside her, a mild smile on his bright red lips. In predawn dark, he lurked beside her like a shadow. When they came to the factory, he presented it to her with a proud wave of his hand, as if he owned it, as if he were the legendary Weber whose name was emblazoned in blue across a placard affixed to the façade. The factory loomed five stories tall, stretched down a block, its high windows glaring with electric light. Through them, she saw men already at work, though the sun was just now surfacing. On top of the building, a thick chimney produced a ragged flag of steam.

Her friend from the tenement ushered her inside the cavernous building and showed her to the business office, where she met the all-important manager: Penzer was his name, a piston of a man, a column of muscle in shirtsleeves and trousers. His face had the look of a machine made of gears and sprockets. It opened and closed its mouth, uttering harsh Polish words of greeting. Her young neighbor had informed her that Penzer was half German, half Polish, but preferred to hire Poles for lower-skilled work, for they cost less and worked harder. So, Karolina spoke to him in Polish. He didn't ask many questions. Had she ever worked in a factory before? Yes, she lied. What sort? She looked at the window and said,
—Glass.

He nodded, as if impressed at the seriousness of this endeavor. Behind him, on the wall over his great desk, a many-sailed schooner fluttered inside its frame. The painted waves crested and fell, a royal ocean blue, and on a shelf beneath this painting, a metronome was ticking ever so slowly, waving its wand at Karolina in a long, graceful arc. Did it always tick and tock as this Penzer worked? Did it measure the time for him in such solemn beats? He wanted to move at a faster tempo. He had agreed to hire her before it had tick-tocked ten times.

Before putting her to work, Penzer gave her a rushed tour of the factory. She struggled to keep up with his gait as he ran down the steps into the basement, where they found a noisy engine room and a shirtless man shoveling coal into the belly of a monstrous furnace. Next door to this was what Penzer called the Drying Room, a dark space kept at a blazing temperature by coils of steam pipes on the walls. Here, dozens of grand piano frames stood in a long line, voluptuously curved, basking in the heat, which, for months, would dry and temper the wood. Besides this room was a much noisier place called the Sawing Room. When Penzer and Karolina entered, the dozen or so men acknowledged the manager with stern nods before resuming their work, which consisted of running planks of timber through saws that sprayed out plumes of fragrant dust. Karolina recognized the smell of spruce.

Upstairs they came to the Regulation Room, where finished instruments were tested and tuned, and here they came upon her young neighbor, hard at work on the upper registers of a baby grand. On the second floor, dozens of workers sat at tables and labored in silence at constructing piano actions. Here, said Penzer, with an air of high respect, the most skilled craftsmen in all the piano industry were at work—German, all German, he said with a wave of the hand over the heads of the men. Above them, more Germans were crafting the all-important sounding boards, made of thin planks glued together, and sanded and planed, sanded and planed, again and again, until the board was but an elegant slip of spruce carved into the shape of a grand piano. In a nearby room, more men worked away at carving piano legs to look like lion's feet, and above them, the entire fourth floor was devoted to constructing the cases. Finally, on the fifth floor, the cases received their varnish in the expansive varnishing room, next door to which was a workshop devoted to the piano keys and hammers. Here, at the top of the grand factory, by windows overlooking the avenue, she was to sit at a table and glue the slender slips of ivory over the keys. This work alone in the factory was given over to women, for it involved no heavy lifting and required, Penzer insisted, a delicate touch.

That day and for many days after she had proven herself adept at the work. She took her place in the row of Polish women with their pots of glue, their keys piled on either side of them, their little stacks of precious ivory. She learned how to brush the glue on the maple, slide the ivory slat into place, and clamp it down—again and again. It was a fine enough place to work. Light poured in from the dusty fifth-floor windows, from which they could see the daily parade along the Avenue, whenever they dared look up from their labor. They did not dare often, for there was always a rush to get more keys ready for more pianos; the factory could not make them fast enough for all the homes that wished to buy them—a Weber baby grand then being the choice ornament for music rooms throughout Manhattan and beyond.

She kept up with the work for months, six days a week, six in the morning til six at night, not missing a day all fall and winter. Then her cousin fell ill. She went to Penzer and begged leave for a few days so she could nurse Marija back to health. His mechanical face twitched and whirred; he made disapproving noises deep in his chest, but to her surprise, he assented: for two days they could manage without her in the Key Room. But two days had passed in a blink. She would have to go today to explain to Penzer what had happened. Beneath his machine exterior thumped a heart infused with family feeling, surely. He'd taken pity on her once and might show yet more leniency if asked.

She stepped away from the flow of foot traffic, leaned against a brick wall to rest beneath an overhang. The snowfall thickened; she could scarcely see the people passing by. It was beautiful how the snow wiped out the city's dinginess, how it filled the broad street with its own light and grace. It felt good to be still, to close her eyes and recall that now it was night in Lietuva, and her children would likely be in bed. She was trying to will herself into their dreams, a tender spirit, a benevolent visitor from afar, when she sensed a rustle of life approaching, the scraping of shoes.

When she opened her eyes, she found two boys standing right in front of her—large boys, thick and strong with stern faces made pink by the cold. They stared at her, not saying a word. The one on the right grabbed hold of both her arms while the other pulled the coin purse out of her hand as if he were picking an apple from a tree. She opened her mouth to call out, but the boy who'd taken the purse smiled at her, and the smile confused Karolina, made her think this was a joke and he'd give the purse back in a moment. Without a word, though, the boys ran off into the crowd.

No one seemed to have noticed. She hadn't made a sound. Her purse with its coins and bills was gone. Follow them, she told herself—stop them; but she simply looked down at her hands, as if to confirm that she hadn't hallucinated the boys taking her purse. Yes, it was gone, gone, all two dollars and thirty-five cents of it—one third a week's pay—no trifling amount, money for her children, gone.

Why hadn't she protested? Why allow those boys to take what they wanted? The audacity of it had shocked her. The silence of their approach, the confidence they'd get what they wanted. The guilt was all hers. She ought not to have rested, to have made herself vulnerable. Now she began to move, reentering the traffic on Delancey. Where had the boys gone? Not far, she guessed, they belonged to the neighborhood, perhaps lived nearby, might still be within shouting distance. Ought she go to the police? How to say *steal? Rob? Theft*? She did not know the most important American words even now.

The will to act dissipated into the sky over Delancey. The rushing crowd, the falling snow, the stacked-up factories overcame her; the city had taken what it needed—her two dollars and thirty-five cents. Who could fight such a hunger as that? The boys were gone. She'd had one instant to resist and had failed to do so. A stronger, braver, fiercer animal might have lashed out, but she'd been thinking—of what? Her children's dreams.

She walked on, wondering how she could buy chamomile now. Might Penzer lend her a dollar? If not, would the man with hair in his ears sell her the tea on credit? He came from her homeland, spoke her language—that went a long way here. He would trust her, she thought, she hoped.

The woman in mourning reappeared in the distance, crossing a street, her black dress hems fluttering over the cobbles. Best not dwell on lost money, Karolina thought. More precious things were in danger now. What was two dollars in a city where death walked the streets in lace?

The crowd on the street had thinned. On this block, only a half dozen or so souls labored through the gale. The woman in black paused, lingered on the walk, gazing at a storefront. Then she walked down a small flight of stairs and disappeared, below street level, through a black door.

A cellar shop—Karolina stood before it, trying to make sense of the lettering on the sign over the door. In a small window she saw books on display. The heat from within had fogged the pane, so that the books appeared shrouded in mystery. Deep in the shop, an electric light burned.

Her errands were pressing. She had been out too long already and was ill besides. Yet how tempting this warm shop looked—a chance to get out of the cold and muse, for a moment, in the company of books. This is why the lady in mourning had appeared, surely, to lead her here, and behind that black door, what turn of destiny might await? What book, containing what secret?

She thought of home, of the long shelves of tomes in the church cellar. She'd read the psalms there once, and a line came to her now like a command: *Be still and know that I am God.*

She opened the door and stepped into the shop, grateful for the sudden warmth and quiet. She saw no one and nothing but books, case after case of them in rows leading into the shop, and between the rows, on the floor, stacks of books that would not fit on the shelves. To her left, a desk with a lit lamp shaded by pink-tinted glass, an empty chair. The shopkeeper must have been helping the woman in black, out of view in the stacks.

    She ventured down a row, her hand moving along the leather spines. When she'd made the book of herbal remedies for the children, she'd struggled with the leather binding. Perhaps it hadn't been supple enough. She hoped it still held together, that the children would look at it and remember her. She stopped at a random place in the row and pulled out a volume not much larger than her hand. It fell open easily. The light was dim, but she held the page up close, smelling the paper and glue. The words were in a language she did not know. A poem— that she could see, and the little black letters imprinted on the soft paper looked somehow tender, as if made of warm substance. She removed her glove and slid her finger over them, as if by touching the words, she might glean their meaning.

    Just then the woman in black appeared at the end of the row. She studied the spines, searching, and then pulled a book into her hands and began to read. Karolina watched her, perplexed by her dark beauty. She had the urge to ask her for help. A foolish whim. What could a stranger give? A coin? A warning? A place to rest? The woman read with a hand over her mouth. Then, at the distant, muffled sound of another church bell, she closed the book and placed it on top of the other volumes on the shelf. She walked down the row toward Karolina and as she passed, she looked her in the eye—a look of familiarity, of intimacy, as if they knew each other. Then she was gone, out the shop door. Her scent remained, though—a scent of old flowers and wool.

Alone, Karolina went to pick up the book the woman had left. It fell open to a page thick with indecipherable prose on the right-hand side, and on the left an illustration: a woman in a crypt, her body shrouded in a white sheet, all of her covered but her face, which bore the expression of one lost to a dream.

The knowledge came with a chill. Today she would die. It felt like certainty. She softly gasped, closed her eyes. She sensed she was floating, out of space and time, released of all duty at last.

But outside, the hour tolled and tolled. It woke her out of her reverie. *What nonsense.* Karolina closed the book and headed to the door.

She ought not to have dawdled in that shop so full of unreadable books. Surfacing again on Delancey, she shivered with cold. The sun hung lower in the sky. Long shadows fell from the bodies of men passing by. Dizzy yet chastened, Karolina walked on, in search of chamomile.

IX

From now on, they could not expect to know what lived behind the closed doors of the world. Here was one: a double door of silvery wood, leading into a monastery. An iron knocker, an iron knob. Beyond this barrier lived men who would or would not be kind. To raise the knocker, to let it fall seemed to Ona a reckless act, necessitated by the fading light.

The knock's faint echo carried over the yard. She looked at her brother. Leaning against the wall, he appeared pale and faint.

The door opened, and there stood a cassocked monk, a pole of a man, skinny and freakishly tall. He was bald and ancient.

—What is this? he said, as if the children were specimens a dog had placed at his feet.

The man had asked a simple question with a complex answer. What is this? What were they? Ona struggled to speak. They needed a place to stay.

The man watched her without saying a word. He pushed open the door wider and showed them inside a stone chamber. He told them in their own tongue to follow him.

They walked down a long hall. They passed door after door and came to a kitchen. A fire burned low in the stove, and there a pot steamed; a monk stood by, stirring. Like the man who'd come to the door, he was elderly, but this monk was short and wore a patch over one eye. The eye that saw looked at the children with astonishment.

—We have company, said the tall monk. Children from the forest. They need food.

He told the children to sit at a long wooden table. The one-eyed monk brought them bowls of stew, and then the tall one asked him to prepare a room for their guests. He went silently away as the children began to eat. The food passed hotly into their stomachs. They ate their portions quickly. When Ona looked up, the tall monk was watching them, the question still in his eyes: What were they doing here? Who were they?

She explained that they'd been sent by Audrius in Varėna, the man who smuggled books. They were on the way to Hamburg, and then to New York, to join their mother and her cousin.

The monk appeared skeptical. He looked at the boy, then the girl, then back at the boy.

—And where are you from?

Ona told him the name of the village.

—And your father?

—He is in America, too.

—But not with your mother?

Ona knew the monk would disapprove of the truth, but she shook her head.

—You can stay here as long as you like, said the man. You'll need to rest. From the looks of you, a bath would help, too.

Now the one-eyed monk came back into the room, his arms stretched nearly to the floor by two buckets of water from the well. He groaned as he eased them to the floor and the two monks worked together to dump the water into a large pot, which they lifted onto the stove to heat.

—Thank you, said Ona. We won't trouble you long. We can leave in the morning.

—You should stay longer. Your brother doesn't look

well, and you have a long way to travel. May I ask why you're in such a hurry?

It wouldn't do to tell the monk that they'd stolen a horse from the police. Ona made up a reason on the spot.

—Our mother is sick.

—God bless her, but if you're not careful, you'll all be sick. It's a hard time of year to travel.

He must think they were foolish runaways, thought Ona, and surely that's what they'd become, but how could they turn back now?

After they'd finished eating and the water had warmed, the monks, carrying the pot between them, led the children down a hall to a room with two cots and a cross on the wall. There was a washbasin, too, and in this they poured the hot water. It steamed clouds in the air, redolent of the well from which it had been pulled. One of the monks brought a rough towel and a lump of soap and then left the children alone.

Once the door had closed, Lukas and Ona collapsed onto the cots, kicked off their boots, and stared at the ceiling. A candle shone on a nightstand between them. The window let in a touch of twilight, but soon that would go, and they would be left to the candle's flame.

—The water's cooling. Get undressed, she told her brother.
—Can't you go first?
—You.

He took off his clothes and stepped into the basin. It was just deep enough so that he could submerge his head by leaning far forward. He wanted to cover all of his body with the hot water, but there wasn't enough, half of him was always exposed. The room was so cold it reminded him of the ride, of the wind cutting into him all day. There would be more cold—whole empires of frigid air outside the walls of this place—and more men with bullets in their guns.

He rose up from the water and saw the crucifix on the wall. It was not the sort his mother had made from reeds—simple and green, hung from nails at Eastertime. On the monks' cross was a bleeding man with a gash in his side. Lukas stared at it darkly.

—My turn, said Ona.

She held the towel open for him, and the boy came into it, grateful for the attention as she rubbed his body warm and red.

Shivering, he huddled under the blankets on his cot as his sister washed. She was changing day by day, growing breasts like his mother, hair between her legs, and he glanced at her with embarrassment, then turned away. Ona saw him looking; it was nothing new, and it had not yet occurred to her to be ashamed. Anyway, she could think only of getting clean and dry. She rushed to rinse the soap off her legs and arms.

Soon they were both under covers on their cots. They spoke in quiet voices.

—Do you think they're really looking for us? he asked his sister.

—If someone stole your horse, would you look for the thief?

—Are we thieves?

She had never thought of herself as such. She was slow to answer.

—I think so, yes.

—We borrowed a horse. The Russians have hundreds, what does it matter?

—It matters if they catch us.

—And what would they do?

—I don't know.

Lukas guessed they would shoot them against a wall. He had heard of Russians doing such things.

With the candle burning its tender light between

them, the children settled in to sleep. Lukas closed his eyes and saw home—the home left behind, the empty bed where he and his sister belonged. In the wood on the wall of their room, right near the place where he would rest his head, the grain swirled around a knot. It resembled a face. Sometimes Lukas called that face God and prayed to it. Of course, he knew that God was not really in the wall; God was everywhere—that's what Lukas's mother had said: like sunlight, He shone on all the earth and made things grow. It didn't matter if you were here or there, north or south, the same God followed you wherever you went. But Lukas still missed his room, which seemed to have more God in it than most places.

He opened his eyes. Night had fallen. His sister was sleeping, he could hear her breathing. He got out of bed and went to find in the satchel their mother's atlas filled with remedies. He brought it back with him to bed, then blew out the candle so that it was all black in the room. Outside, snow was falling—the flakes came slow and gentle in the dark, and he watched them, mesmerized. Beyond the monastery yard was forest—thick and dark and boundless. New York was impossibly far away. He curled under the covers with the book beside him, smelling from inside its folded pages so many scents of home—angelica, carraway, chamomile.

Hours later, a loud knock on the bedroom door woke the children. They opened their eyes, thinking they were still home. Then, hearing another knock, they remembered their journey. Ona sat up with a start, bracing herself for danger, as the door slowly opened.

It was the monk with the eye-patch. He smiled.

—Good morning, he said. It's time for prayers.

He waited as the children dressed in silence. Their clothes were stiff with cold; they smelled of winter and horse. The monk led the guests down a hall toward a pair of doors painted blue. They passed through them into a small stone chapel with an altar draped in gray linen. On the dais knelt five monks in a row, heads bowed. The cross over the altar was made of two logs nailed together. There were three rows of simple plank benches, and the one-eyed monk directed them to wait in the back until they were finished.

So, they sat in a daze, watching their breath, listening to the sound the monks made praying to God. They said nothing aloud, but their very presence on the altar, those five large men in robes, made some blue noise in the cold—the sound of human concentration, a low whir, as if a breeze were moving through the room. Why had they been summoned here? Ona presumed they were expected to pray, and so, being obedient, she put her hands together and began, in silence, to rehearse the Hail Mary, the words of which her mother had taught her. It was difficult to concentrate. God had always been real the way the houses of her village were. They had been part of her world, you saw them without noticing them, and could always count on their presence. Now that she'd left the village, now that she'd stolen a horse, and both her parents were on the other side of the ocean, the idea of God had changed. It was no longer like a house at all, but like a memory of a day gone by.

Lukas didn't pray. He was trying to remember a dream he'd been having when the knock on the door woke him. It had involved horses—a herd of them running across a grassy field. One of them was his, he knew, and he needed to catch her—but when he tried to get close, the horses swerved toward him and charged. He ran for his life into a forest, but the hoof-beats gained, and his little legs slowed—soon the beasts would be upon him. As the memory came back to him, his heart began to pound. He sidled closer to his sister, whose mouth was moving in silence.

Now the monks rose to their feet with creaking knees and sighs. The tall elderly monk whom they'd met last night came to sit near the children.

—Are you well-rested?

Ona said that they were.

—We've fed and watered your horse. He'll be ready when you are. Do you still want to go?

Ona was about to say yes when they all heard noise from outside the chapel. They looked out the tall narrow windows, and there, in the yard, three horsemen came sauntering—police in uniform, with sabers at their side, rifles strapped to their backs, and beaver hats on their heads.

Ona grabbed the monk's hand and looked into his eyes.

—We need to hide.

—But why?

—Please!

The monk asked no more questions. He held Ona's hand as he led her toward the back of the chapel. He opened a narrow door in the corner, exposing a staircase that descended into a musty cellar.

The stairway led to a long narrow room lined with tombs. The monk pulled matches from his pocket beneath his robes and used them to light a half-melted candle affixed to the wall. He walked them further into the crypt and knelt to pull a stone slab from a wall, revealing a cavity large enough for a small coffin.

—Do you really need to hide?

The children looked into the dark space. They could hear voices above. Ona nodded.

—I'll get you as soon as they're gone. Hurry.

Ona clambered in first, sliding to the back of the tomb. Lukas got in beside her. They curled together, as if in a bed, on the rough, cold stone.

—Don't be afraid, said the monk. If you run out of air, push the stone away and get out.

The monk lifted the stone with a grunt and wedged it back into position.

The children were accustomed to darkness. They had known the darkness of moonless winter nights, of lightless outhouses, even of cellars. But this darkness was deeper, fiercer—it corkscrewed into their eyes. Lukas began to cry. Ona held his hand and cooed into his ear: *calm down, be strong*. His fingers reached toward the ceiling, their tips grazed the top. It was damp and jagged.

He reached out to feel the smooth stone slab blocking the light.

—We could die here, he whispered.

—We won't. They'll tell the officers to go away, and then they'll come for us.

—I want to get out.

—Not yet. Shut your eyes and pretend you're somewhere else.

He tried to imagine they were in the hayloft back home, where moonlight would seep through cracks between boards in the walls. There the hay smelled of the summer sun, and a feral cat with bright eyes would sometimes prowl—so that even in the darkest nights, it never seemed so very black, and they could always find their way by touch. Sometimes in warm weather, they would sleep in the loft, the two children, with their mother, to get away from the sound of their uncle's snoring, and then she would tell them tales or sing songs or simply listen to an owl in the woods—and when it grew cold, they would snuggle in close like rabbits. Lukas would shut his eyes and imagine all the creatures prowling and flitting about in the brush not far from the barn—the foxes and mice, the deer and hedgehogs—all of them serenely threading the dark. Now, in the crypt, he tried to bring all this back to his mind, but the smell of the damp stone interfered; he knew too well where he was. His thoughts turned to his father.

In his most secret imaginings, Lukas admitted to himself the man might be buried somewhere in America. That would explain the silence and neglect. And if his father was dead and buried, would he know it was so? Would he lie in his grave wishing he were standing upright in the sun? This did not seem possible. Then again, you didn't stop thinking after you died, and your body—your body would be here, in a place as black, as damp, as closed in as this, and you would want to scream with all your might to be free, you would want that, anyone would—it's what Lukas wanted now, even as his sister clutched at his hand, for she said she heard footsteps.

Yes, footsteps, very faint, somewhere above them? Or beside them? Maybe this was the way the dead heard the living—a rumor of life imagined through stone walls. Outside, the sun would be rising, the horses standing in the snow-covered yard, the birds singing in the trees. Ona thought of all these things, and then of the cross in the chapel upstairs, where the officers were likely traipsing about, searching for them. At the sound of a footstep, she made the mistake of opening her eyes, and the blackness of the tomb twisted inside her, so that she cried aloud.

Yes, footsteps, the weight of men making the beams groan. A prayer moved through Ona like a cold wind—not to God, nor Mary, nor any saint, but to her mother, the memory of her—a prayer aching with longing for all good things.

Then the stone began to move. It made a rough, scraping sound. A wedge of light fell on their faces. There stood two monks holding the slab, smiling at the entombed children.

Lukas scrambled out first, and Ona came next, more slowly and carefully. The monks led the children upstairs through the chapel, down a long hall, to the kitchen where they'd eaten the night before. The other monks they'd seen in the chapel sat at the table, breakfasting on bread and a round of cheese and tea.

—Make room for our fugitives, said the tallest, most elderly of the men. His companions obeyed, and the children sat down with them, all too conscious of their guilt.

—So, tell us now all about the horse, my dear, said the old monk.

—Audrius gave it to us, said Ona at once.

—And how did you get to Audrius' house in Varėna?

She thought of telling them that they'd walked, but the lie stuck in her throat.

—Horse theft is a serious crime, said the monk. We told them we knew nothing of your whereabouts, but they didn't believe us. They said they'd be back, and next time we might not be so lucky.

After breakfast, the one-eyed monk took them into a cellar and invited the children to fill the empty space in their bags with apples, smoked sausage, and cheese. Another monk brought out Audrius' colt and helped the children into the saddle. To the west and east stretched the main road, down which the police had traveled. To the southwest, their narrower road continued winding inconspicuously through the woods.

Ona gently pressed her heels against the flanks of the colt, and the beast sprang forward. She looked back and saw the worried face of the old monk, the sunlight on the cross atop the chapel, and the white monastery where they'd played at being dead. Then she turned away, and the horse carried them further down the trail so that soon there was no sign of that place, and no sign of any building or settlements at all, and they were again hidden in the vast woods.

X

The city was astonished with snow. It had dusted all fire escapes and sills, lampposts and roofs, the tops of men's hats. Karolina walked west with new purpose, eager to reach the Weber factory, hopeful that Penzer would grant her wishes. They were unusual, to be sure—more days off, a bit of advance pay—but the city granted miracles to ordinary people every day, and she believed in blessings.

She covered the distance from Delancey to Seventh in what seemed like no time at all. For all the tedium of gluing ivory onto piano keys hour after hour, six long days a week, she still was not beyond feeling proud of the factory. She stood before it now, admiring its ornate façade, behind which even more ornate creations were being crafted. Up high, near the top of the building, three naked Atlas figures held up the roof with strong arms, and next to the middle god was the window where Karolina would sit with her glue pot and brush.

She crossed the avenue and entered the factory doors. The building smelled all over of freshly sawed lumber, varnish, glue—a pleasing, civilized smell of high achievement. Near the front doors was a newly created showroom for the highest-end Weber pianofortes. The quickest way to Penzer's office went through it—a rich room, with shiny wood floors, luxuriously papered walls, and a high ceiling from which hung a crystal chandelier, with its new electric lights. People had come inside the showroom just to see the chandelier, so impressive was the ornament used to illuminate the merchandise below. Though to call these grand pianos merchandise was to cheapen them. They were works of art, with ornate, polished mahogany cases and lion's claw feet. The center piano even had painted panels on its side—landscapes of mountains, streams, and wooded valleys. Karolina had never learned to play the piano, she couldn't even read music, yet she coveted these objects all the same, for she could see how elegant they were and knew what they signified: civilization, refinement, success. She liked to think that when she passed through these years of toil and drudgery, arriving into her more genuine life, her prosperity to come, she would somehow acquire one of these machines. She would install one in her parlor so that her children could learn to play. If not her children, then her grandchildren. If not them, her great grandchildren, for Karolina hoped to live long. No matter the price of the finest pianofortes, no matter that she did not have enough money to pay for her children to cross the ocean—her desire ran along a higher, freer plane, without care for ordinary human roads. She lingered here, taking the chance to sit on a bench, to hold her hands over the keys that she'd helped assemble and imagine the freedom of summoning music into the air with her fingers.

A salesman appeared from behind a curtain in the back of the room, and asked in a censorious voice,

—May I help you?

Karolina pulled her hand away as if it'd been bitten. She stepped away from the instrument.

—I work here, she said in her stiff English. I need Penzer.

—Workers are not allowed in the showroom. Come with me.

The salesman—a tall man in a suit and polished black

shoes that clicked importantly on the floor—led her through the curtains in the back of the room, into a dark hallway that came to Penzer's office. He knocked twice on the door and, hearing no answer, took the liberty of opening it to confirm that Penzer was not there.

—He must have gone up to the sawing room. Take the back stairs.

Karolina understood only the phrase *sawing room*, but that was enough. She took her leave of the salesman and headed to a stairwell at the other end of the hall. She walked down the stairs, shocked to have been treated so rudely by the salesman. She'd never accepted being a second-class citizen. What about her told the world she was an outsider and so to be dismissed? Her English? Her dowdy clothes or hesitant manner? But surely it was all these things, and she felt ashamed as she made her way into the sawing room in the factory basement.

Here were rows of worktables on which men measured and sawed strips and blocks and planks of lumber for the construction of the piano's many wooden parts. She stood near the doorway, watching the men labor in silence. Their shirts were stained with sweat, though it was cool in the room. They were bent over their work, so absorbed that no one noticed Karolina for minutes, and all that time she watched them lend their bodies to the task. She liked the sharp scent of lumber and sweat, the sight of their forearms sprinkled with sawdust.

At last, one of the men saw her, put down the saw in his hands, and came to her.

—Is something the matter? he said in Polish.

—I'm looking for Penzer. Do you know where he is?

—You missed him. He went upstairs—to varnishing, I think.

—Oh, good. Thank you.

—You don't seem well. Are you sick?

Karolina ignored the question and turned up the stairway. As she climbed to the fifth floor, each flight tired her. She stopped often to catch her breath and steady her dizziness. Her face was still hot, yet she felt cold to her bones and sore in the joints. Still, she climbed, and the youth who'd helped her find the job came down the other direction. Seeing her, he paused, nodded warily, and hurried on. Was he afraid of her? Of catching the grippe? Fear pervaded the city; it made the factory move, made the bodies show up and bend to the task as required by bosses who did not care what became of you. Penzer, though—Penzer was a good Polish boy; he'd be good to Karolina simply because he had no reason not to be, she hoped.

She reached the fifth floor at last. On one side of the landing was the varnishing room. On the other side, the key room where she worked. She didn't want to face her fellow workers now; they would wonder why she wasn't where she belonged. She would have to explain all about her cousin's illness, her search for chamomile, her unreasonable cross-town journey. But if she had been replaced, it would be easy enough to find out, she could see as much at a glance through the doorway, and so she chanced a look.

She had never seen her co-workers this way, from the outside peering in. How skilled and absorbed they looked in the light washing in from the windows, their heads bowed, hands busy with wooden keys and brushes and ivory. The air in the room smelled of glue and made Karolina feel faint. In the place where she usually sat, another girl had appeared who looked quite like Karolina—fair-haired, pale, slender; she even tilted her head to the side as Karolina would sometimes do.

To lose your place was a disaster—everyone thought so. You clung to any opportunity fate gave you; if you lost it, you could starve; people went hungry in the streets for want of work.

Karolina returned to the landing and crossed into the great hall where workers applied varnish to new piano cases. Three new cases were being worked on, and in the back of the room stood Penzer, imperious, yelling in Polish at his workers; they were behind schedule, they needed to be more efficient; more pianos were coming this afternoon, and they would not be allowed to leave before they were finished. The tirade put fear into the men; Karolina could see it in their faces, the acceleration of their movements. She waited by the doorway in her coat and hat, concentrating on Penzer, willing him to give her what she desired. Eventually, he stopped talking and walked self-importantly across the room toward the exit. Only then did he notice her.

—Mr. Penzer.

—You!

—Yes, I've come to ask you for help.

He looked confused.

—My cousin is still sick, she said. She needs someone to care for her. That's why I haven't been to work this week. You must have family, too, Mr. Penzer, and understand what it means to be in this position.

She had not spoken so much in days; the words came thickly in her throat. Her voice sounded strange to her.

—I'll come back to work as soon as she's better, she insisted. Please don't give away my place.

—We already have.

—I can do some other work then—

—We don't have need.

—I'll work twice as hard.

—It isn't necessary, dear.

—I promise—

—Please don't be foolish—you have no place any longer. I'm sorry, but this is a business. If workers don't show up, we replace them.

—Please, sir—I have no money.

She had never begged in her life, but it came easily, and the plaintive note in her voice worked some magic on Penzer. He reached into his pocket and pulled out a dime.

—You know I'm a good worker, I'll come back and make up for the lost time—

He put the dime in her hand, walked by her, and rushed down the stairs.

She did not completely believe that she'd lost her place; the injustice of it was too flagrant. She'd go home, nurse Marija to health, then return to the factory. If the stronger, prettier version of Karolina now sitting in the key room was still in her chair—well, they could always find another chair, for weren't they under tremendous pressure to produce more and more keys for more and more pianos? They could not possibly kick Karolina out altogether over a case of the grippe.

Even so, as these certitudes moved through her mind, on a lower level, well below her waking thoughts, crept the knowledge that none of this mattered: a more urgent task than making keys and money awaited her; more necessary human work was at hand.

—Chamomile, she thought, looking at the shiny dime in her palm.

She put it in her pocket and took one last look at the workers gathered round their instruments, brushing the varnish onto the cases room. This factory would do just fine without her. The machinery would go on grinding out the instruments as fast as people bought them.

As she turned to go, spots swam in the corners of her vision. Descending, she held tight to the stairway railing. She could hear all around her the factory's commotion— its hammering and sawing, sanding and scraping, men shouting as they heaved and dropped pallets of lumber. Below, inside Penzer's office, she knew, the old metronome waved on, marking the days into slow beats, each beat a dollar, each dollar a hope, a desire sublimated into the great machines, one of which was being played now in the showroom. Reaching the foyer at the bottom of the staircase, Karolina paused to listen.

What was that golden music? She couldn't say, but how lovely, this rich, rippling fabric of sound! She leaned against a dusty wall, listening, eyes closed, gathering that distant music around her like a warm coat. She wanted to take it with her into the streets, to keep it close inside.

She pushed open the heavy factory doors and stepped onto Seventh Avenue, where the light was beginning to fade. It was late afternoon, and the market would be closing soon. Time was running out.

XI

The forest was a frozen world sealed from time. They moved through it as trespassers. They saw no birds, no squirrels or deer, yet an invisible presence brooded in the shadows. There were no eyes to see them, yet the children on their colt felt watched all the same, accounted for by the forest in the early morning hours.

They were grateful when the sun rose higher, broke through the clouds, and dispelled the stillness. Lukas was relieved enough to say aloud,

—Let's call him Chocolate.

He meant the colt, and Ona agreed. Thus named, Chocolate seemed to them more amiable and trustworthy. Lukas patted his flank, telling him he was a good boy and that he'd soon have an apple.

At midday, they came to an oak growing out of the trail. Beyond it, more trees blocked the way, or what ought to have been the way. Ona pulled at the reins, looked around, peering into the woods, seeing no sign of a trail in the thicket. Then she spied a gap between two pines; she led Chocolate between them, down a slope, and for a time Ona felt confident they'd regained the trail—until trees again impeded their way.

Ona watched the colt's breath unfurl in the cold air. She led them back to the oak. There, Lukas spied another gap in the trees, off in a different direction, and they tried that way, too, but again found themselves daunted by an expanding maze of trees, with no clear path ahead.

They returned to the oak and tried a third way, on the other side of a fallen trunk. This, too, led them into snowy bramble, and the forest seemed more enormous than ever, as a wind blew through it.

They went back again and dismounted from Chocolate. They fed him two apples and cut open one of the monks' cheeses. They ate in silence as branches around them trembled, and clumps of melting snow fell from limbs. The forest was astir with rumors that had nothing to do with their little lives, which could end soon enough, they knew, if they let themselves get lost in the depths of winter.

While they waited, wondering what to do, they heard the soft sound of a horse's steps approaching. Their first thought: hide—but how to hide with a colt leaving footprints in the snow? Then: run—but where to run to? So they stayed where they were, hoping that whoever was coming would be one of their own.

Soon a slow-footed, sand-colored horse appeared through the trees. It was pulling a wooden sleigh in which sat an old man in a fur cap and coat. He halted his horse and greeted the children in a loud, rough voice.

—What brings you this way?

—We're heading to the border, Ona said, but we've lost the way.

The man narrowed his eyes, looking from Ona to Lukas to Chocolate, and back to Ona again. His face was a bright red color and chapped with weather, his grey eyebrows traced with frost.

—Follow me, he said. We're not far from home.

The man in the sleigh led them down the way they'd first tried, but then veered left, through a gap in the trees that had escaped their notice. Here, the trail became so obvious and clear, that Ona could only smile.

In less than an hour they came to a village hushed by open sky, ringed by forest. A frozen stream wound through it. There were only three houses, two barns, icicles dripping off their eaves like lashes. It was a relief to see an open swath of sky again, to see smoke rising from chimneys and polite fences crossing a field. A small black dog raced through the powdery snow toward the sleigh. The man whistled at the dog and gave him a treat from his pocket as they approached one of the houses.

—Come, he told the children as he got out of his sleigh. Let me take your horse.

The children dismounted, and the man led Chocolate to one of the barns. He installed the colt in a stable there, beside a thin dairy cow. With a pitchfork, the man fed their horse a heap of hay from a pile and told Ona to bring water from the well in the yard. She did so, and they listened as their colt drank noisily from the wooden bucket. Then, after providing for their animal, the man stabled his own horse, fed it and watered it, and they finally went inside the house.

There, in the dark room, they found a small, plump woman with a gently wrinkled face. She observed the strangers in her doorway with a hint of fear in her eyes.

—I picked them up on the way home from the lake.

They said they're headed for the border.
—But where are their parents?
—America, Lukas said. We're going there, too.
The man and woman looked at each other. The woman protested:
—You're too young for such a journey.
Her husband disagreed. Her sister's son, not much older than Ona, had run off to America with his bride just last year. And wasn't he doing fine?
—But he's a man, said his wife.
—He's a boy, and foolish.
The man looked at Lukas and Ona as if assessing their mettle.
—Well, let's get you something to eat.

He'd been ice-fishing in a nearby lake. The three fish he'd brought in his sleigh his wife quickly gutted and fried in melted butter and garlic. She put out conserved mushrooms and cucumbers and sweet tomatoes, and she fried sliced potatoes, too, and served all this feast on a table draped in linen. By the time they all sat down to eat, the children knew they were more than welcome, that the old man and woman were glad to have someone to cook for, in the middle of a long, quiet winter.

The man asked the children where in America their parents were living.

—New York, said Ona.

The name of the city had a curious effect on the old man's face. He looked neither impressed nor disappointed, and not quite confused, yet it seemed to Ona that she'd uttered a sound the man could not understand, nor had any need to, yet which subtly peeved him. New York was not a good answer, it seemed—at least, not an answer to which he could give any response. He turned his attention to the fish on his plate.

—How much further is it to the border? asked Ona then.

—If you set out before dawn, you'll reach it tomorrow evening.

—Are you sure you want to go? the woman asked.

The question sounded not entirely unlike a plea—a plea to stay? Perhaps with them, a childless couple? Would they adopt the children, make them their own? A vision came to Ona in a flash, a vision of life peacefully unfurling year by year on this farm, with strangers for parents providing all the food and comfort a body could need. The notion chilled her, warned her against what would come if they stayed behind—a future bereft of their mother.

—Yes, her brother answered when she failed to. We're sure.

They said little else over dinner. After eating, while the woman was cleaning up, the man invited the children into the yard. It was a cold, clear night. Smoking a pipe, he looked up at the stars and gestured toward them, as if they were his to share. There were thousands upon thousands of stars swimming in the black sky.

—In New York, do they have stars like this? he muttered.

The children gawked up, heads tilted far back, as streaks of light began to race through the heavens. One after another, stars travelled in glittering arcs down the curtain of night.

—Why are the stars falling? asked Lukas in a whisper.

—They do that sometimes, said the man.

—Why?

They all stood in the cold with the question ringing in their ears.

Soon the movement in the heavens stopped. All was fixed. A half-moon called out. A dog nearby barked back at it. The man sighed, and his pipe smoke smelled delicious.

—They do have stars in New York, Ona said quietly. There are stars all over.

The man looked down and smiled at her as if withholding a secret he could not share.

—You'll see, he said. You'll see what kind of stars are there, won't you?

The man's wife used some spare blankets to make a bed on the floor in the kitchen—the warmest room in the house, she said. Then she and the man went to bed, leaving the children alone. Not yet sleepy, Lukas and Ona sat against the wall for a time, listening to the wood burn in the furnace. A candle on the table cast light on their faces. There wasn't much of the candle left, only a flickering nub. Lukas brought out his pencil and paper and began to draw its flame surrounded by darkness. As he worked, he asked his sister what time it was in New York. She said she didn't even know the time here.

—Do you think everyone in New York always knows the time?

—I couldn't say.

—Do they all have watches in their pockets?

—I couldn't say that either.

—I think they do, said Lukas.

He drew for a time without saying anything. The pencil made a pleasing sound on the page. The candle was coming along nicely. It was satisfying to create the semblance of light with nothing but lead on paper.

—I suppose it's still night in New York now, he mused. Almost morning. Mamytė must still be sleeping.

—Yes.

—I hope Marija is still with her.

—I'm sure she is, she said.

—How do you know?

—I don't actually.

Lukas put down his pencil and shut his eyes. Ona closed her eyes, too. They both floated in the dark, feeling the warmth of the furnace on their faces. They could hear the fire's gentle hiss and snap, and Lukas fancied it was the sound of angels talking, passing their prayers on to God.

But when he opened his eyes again, the candle's flame had guttered out.

XII

Light-headed and pale, Karolina moved into the avenue. It rolled away southward, a vast expanse, chaotic with horses and carts.

The man she sought made his living in Gansevoort Market selling dried herbs, honey, and mushrooms foraged from forests outside the city. He had a deep tan, a handsome face, and a bald head ringed with tufts of brilliant white hair in which twigs and leaves were often caught. Quick as a squirrel, a fast talker, he had small rapid hands that restlessly fondled jars of honey when he was eager to make a sale. Built low to the ground, he was at ease in forests; on this continent or his own, he could find chanterelles after a hard rain, wild blueberries, nettles for soup. Karolina envied his connection to the environs outside the city, which she could scarcely imagine when cooped up inside her factory or tenement home. Yet this man, equipped with horse and cart, ventured into unspoiled tracts of woodlands to find mushrooms in the shadows of oaks and sycamores—precious forest gold. They'd met a few months back, while she was browsing the market in search of honey one day after work. Lacking the English word for honey, she simply pointed at one of the jars and tried asking for it in Russian.

—Where are you from? he asked in the same tongue, handing her the jar she'd pointed out.

—Two days journey from Vilna, she said.

He smiled and began to speak to her in her mother tongue. It was like discovering an old friend. She wanted to kiss him. They talked a long time as shoppers milled around them. She learned that he'd been baptized in the same church as her mother. His wife had died the year before, and he now lived with a nephew and his family in Yonkers. She told him about her cousin Marija, her job in the piano factory up the road, how much she missed her children. She happily bought two jars of honey and a bag of dried chamomile from the old man, whose name she failed to learn, and promised to return when she needed more.

She turned west onto 14th, into the sinking sun. How had this day so swiftly escaped her? Marija seemed far away, as if it would take years to get back to her side, when it was only a matter of blocks. In her pocket, her hand squeezed Penzer's dime; it was the truth about this day—down to the last borrowed cents.

Turning south on Hudson, she saw a black umbrella ahead. It couldn't be the same woman? But it did look like her—the same black coat, hat, umbrella floating along through the dingy crowd. She quickened her pace to catch up, to get a better glimpse. She began to gain on her, as if the woman were scarcely moving, and then, in a moment, Karolina was at her side. She turned to look and saw that it was an old woman, someone entirely different, with a dry colorless face and stringy gray hair showing from beneath her hat. Karolina turned away, disappointed beyond reason.

She soon came into the sprawling marketplace. In warmer months, the square would be filled with wagons heaped with fruits and vegetables, but now it was mostly empty; the few carts remaining offered old apples, potatoes, carrots, heads of cabbage with browning leaves.

The horses stomped and shifted their feet in the cold dust. She looked about for her friend and saw him in his usual place, in front of the entrance to the poultry house—the indoor market where live chickens could be butchered before your eyes. Here it smelled unpleasantly of blood and gore, but the man preferred the spot, for those who could afford meat could likewise afford wild mushrooms and honey. She approached him from behind, touched his shoulder, so that he spun around.

—Oh!

His face said it plainly: she must have looked quite ill. He at once asked what had happened, what was wrong.

—We need more chamomile, she said.

—I have it.

He pushed jars of honey and conserved mushrooms on the back of his cart out of the way, climbed spryly into it, and pulled a crate out from beneath a blanket. Here, hidden away, was the thing she'd come for: a bundle of dried flowers in a little burlap sack. Why did she believe in its power? Only now did she question the old home remedy, which had in the past seemed so necessary. Here, in this new place, with its mysterious germs and contagions, its millions of strangers, would the simple tea of a chamomile flower cool the fever as it had seemed to at home? To place faith in such frail blessings seemed foolish now. But Karolina held out her dime all the same.

—I won't take a cent. Take it, go home, get warm, you look awful, my dear, you need rest.

He betrayed some skittishness as he held out the sack of flowers. He, too, was worried he'd catch the grippe, wasn't he? She took the offering and thanked him. She wanted to tell him something more, but it was getting late, she had to get back. She turned to go, and then stopped, for he'd called to her.

—Take some of my honey with you, Karolina!

She looked at the old man holding out his gift. How good of him to have remembered her name! The terrible certainty she'd felt in the bookstore struck her again: she would not survive this illness. She'd never see him again, nor the square with all its horses and carts. This dingy marketplace and everyone in it—they too would vanish. She took in the sight: an old woman fingering a withered head of cabbage, a pile of bruised pears dusted with snow, a black-coated man maneuvering over cobbles with his cane, heaps of mud-strewn potatoes, windows pooling light, and the warm dark spaces in so many human mouths opening and closing, calling out prices—it was too much to disappear. How could it do so?

—Do you need honey, Karolina?

  She did. She took it, muttered her thanks, and turned toward home.

She walked steadily east, the setting sun at her back. Her shadow and that of others rose in a thicket over the cold ground. They walked, all of them together, as if to their deaths, Karolina thought, for she could not be the only one—some of them must have it, too? But they did not; they walked more resolutely than she, their slim black shadows gliding by her own like ships on a current. She wanted to lie down. After walking several blocks, she let herself rest against a lamppost.

  As if from nowhere, a man appeared at her side. His bland, mild, unreadable face turned toward Karolina as he said something gently deferential in English. He held out his arm. She took it, realizing as she did so that this was the man with the pocket watch she'd seen earlier. Why did she trust him now? She had not understood what he'd said to her but for one word: *help*.

  For a long time, they walked and said nothing. She kept her arm linked through his, and he laid his other hand over her forearm as they progressed, so that they might have appeared to be lovers. Feeling conspicuous,

Karolina said,

—Everyone is looking at us.

She uttered these words in her mother's language so, of course, he could not have understood. Still, he smiled with irony and pleasure and replied in a low, confidential voice, so that Karolina felt not only that she'd been understood, but that she'd been appreciated, too.

—But you haven't told me why you are following me, she replied. I would like to know.

She wanted to trust him, and it was easy to do so, to relinquish herself to his guidance. He walked at a nice, slow pace, did not demand conversation, and seemed—by virtue of his nearness, his presumption—to know a great deal about her. That familiarity, inexplicable as it was, comforted her as they made their way around a patch of frozen ice on the ground.

Dusk was coming on, the puddles were freezing over, and the lateness of the hour recalled to her mind the doctor's address in her pocket. She took out the card given to her by the grieving mother in her building and showed it to him. It read:

Pietr Sadowski, Medical Doctor
26 MacDougal Street

The man looked at it, at her, and nodded with

assurance, understanding at once, it seemed, that she wished to be escorted there. When they came to the corner of 14th and Sixth Avenue, they turned south.

They went the rest of the way in silence. She felt grateful and could not understand why she'd ever distrusted his intentions. She had begun to assume that they were benevolent. He'd appeared as if summoned by some inner desperation and had provided her what was required—a supportive arm to lean on as she made her way eastward. She liked his abiding silence as they walked, the companionship of it, the way he put his gloved hand over her arm.

Had she been tricked? Cities were predatory places, and hunters were devious; they knew well how to fool their prey. She understood as much, but the knowledge was abstract. What gave her conviction was the body, and her body felt comfort in the stranger's presence. She leaned on him. When he began to speak to her, as they made their way down the avenue, she had the impression she'd been here before, with him, on this very block, walking past an old, red-faced beggar with his mongrel dog shivering in the cold. It was as if she were reliving a dream. What was the man saying? She didn't even try to understand, the words washed over her. Maybe he was telling a story. A story about his life. But it did not seem possible that he had a past at all, that he had a home, or a life beyond his connection to her, so completely was his attention devoted to Karolina now.

They had come to the address on the card, a townhouse with a shingle out front that advertised the doctor's name in bold, black letters.

—Thank you, she told the man in English, taking her arm out of his, and turning to go into the house.

—You are most welcome, he replied before turning to leave her once more to her own devices.

XIII

The moon still hung overhead as the children prepared to leave the old couple's home. The man stood in the yard, patting the colt's neck as they mounted and felt the beast shift beneath them. Scarfs of breath unspooled from the horse's nose. The frigid air smarted their cheeks. Their backs and bottoms already ached from their long travels, and the road awaiting them, they knew, would tax them.

At breakfast, feeding the children thick slices of ham cooked in fat, the woman had said to them,

—It's a long trip to the border. It could be dark by the time you arrive. You could wait a few days, get more rest. It would be better for you. You see we have room.

They had felt good in their beds, beside the furnace, and the ham tasted rich in their mouths. The invitation tempted them terribly. But Ona told the woman what she believed to be true:

—Our mother is waiting for us.

Even as she said this, she felt it to be more wish than fact. The old couple did not seem convinced, but they helped them prepare to leave.

Before they set off, the woman joined the man in the yard. They stood side-by-side as Chocolate began to walk toward the woods. When the children looked back, the woman raised her hand in a wave. They appeared to be frozen in time, small and brave in the predawn dark. Before their colt had reached the road, the woman called out:

—Be strong!

Their strength: more wish than fact. They trembled with cold in the moonlit woods. They did not speak, for fear of shattering the precious quiet and making their presence known to whatever menace lurked in the bramble.

As they rode, Lukas rested his cheek on his sister's back. He closed his eyes, trusting her, trusting the horse, the road. The future had become their new home. There was no other way. He remembered the stars falling the night before, and the man doubting that New York had such marvels, and his sister contradicting him, and the man saying they would see, they would see what sort of stars watched over New York.

—What did he mean? asked Lukas. What did he mean about the stars?

—I don't know, said Ona.

—Aren't the stars the same everywhere?

—Yes, she said.

—And the moon. And the sun. And other things, too.

They had walked several minutes before Ona asked him,

—What other things?

Lukas wasn't sure.

—Just the way things are, he tried. Potatoes, say—a potato here and there, the same. Apples. And trees, and roads, and people.

—I don't think it's the same at all, she said. Otherwise, why would people leave one place to go to another?

His sister was right. The man, too, most likely. He felt nervous. And his back hurt, and he could not feel his toes in his boots.

Nor could he feel his fingers in his mittens by the time they reached the border. They saw it from a distance, across a wide field ringed with forest. On the far side, fencing blocked the way of the road, and a cadre of guards in uniform milled about in the cold. Seeing them far ahead, the children remained in the shadow of the woods.

If they crossed the border along this road, they could be apprehended for the theft of the horse. Children traveling alone, they were too conspicuous. So, earlier that morning, as the man in the village had filled their satchels to bursting with apples and bread, Ona had shyly asked how one might cross without being noticed. He'd looked at them darkly and said that the only way would be through the forest, which was thick and patrolled by guards on the lookout for smugglers. They would need to go slow on their horse through the thicket a long way to the south before turning west and making a run for it.

—How will we know we're on the other side?

—You won't at first, but then you'll hit fields, and due north you'll find the town across the border.

Now they obeyed the old man's instructions. They turned off the trail into the woods, where the snow was deeper. Chocolate's legs sank up to his knees. He proceeded carefully and soon they were surrounded by pines and birch. Evening was coming on fast. They tried their best to be quiet. Wind-rustle and bird-call punctured the silence. With each step further in, Ona could sense danger's nearness.

Then, far ahead, or perhaps behind them, came voices: men talking idly, in Russian. The children kept on, trying not to make a sound. Soon the voices faded, and all was quiet again. Ona turned Chocolate to the right, in the direction she believed was west.

They rode ten minutes more before hearing the jingle of a harness nearby. Then, at the crack of a gunshot, Chocolate burst forward, a jolt of frightened speed, and they ran headlong through the woods, ducking branches. A man's voice called out behind them, and then another to their right. A second shot rang out, and just ahead, a tree trunk splintered. Chocolate surged faster, Ona clung to him, and Lukas clung to her, fearful of falling off the horse, whom they could no longer control. More shots rang out, as a second pursuer appeared to their right, a guard on horseback aiming his rifle.

The children bent low as the shot flew overhead. Lukas screamed as though he'd been hit; it was only a branch whipping his face, making it bleed, as the colt bolted through the last of the woods into an open field. Under a dusky sky, the fugitives raced on, kicking the colt's sides with their heels. Behind them, the guards reared up at the forest's edge, leveled their guns and fired two shots that winged with some angel's grace away from the children, who gasped great gulps of terror in their throats.

The colt ran on, over furrowed earth, hooves thudding, kicking up snow. Tears of cold streamed off the cheeks of the children, the world looked bleary, a wash of red sky and ice. More gunfire echoed across the vast distance. Lukas turned back to see; the guards remained at the wood's edge, watching the children go.

Following the old man's advice, they rode north until they came to the town.

In the new country, the sky looked wider and darker than in their own; the roads stretched into vaster distances than any they had known before. They waited on their exhausted horse in the center of a town square, wondering where to turn.

An old woman appeared. Hidden in scarves, her back bent, she shuffled along with a cane to a small building covered with snow—a store, it seemed from its shingle. Through the frosted window, a young clerk looked out at the children. They dismounted from the colt, tied him to a post, and followed the old woman inside.

Here, in the yellow light of a lamp, the woman had already made her requests, and the clerk was taking down a tin from a high shelf. He opened it and began removing heaps of dried flowers for tea. The woman began to cough, a deep rumbling cough that roughly shook her body. The boy said something to her in a dialect the children failed to understand. In her mind, Ona began forming a good Polish sentence, a simple declarative statement that could be acted on.

When the old woman had paid her coins for the tea and the clerk had turned his attention to Lukas and Ona, she told him,

—We want to sell our horse.

He squinted at her in confusion, so she repeated herself, enunciating the words slowly and clearly. Looking skeptical, the clerk went to the window to examine their so-called horse.

—Sell your horse? he said.

She nodded, feeling foolish and ashamed to be so ignorant of how the world worked.

—Why?

—We need the money.

—How much?

Back in Varèna, Audrius had said they might fetch

seventy marks for the colt. Ona said eighty, and the clerk gave her a cunning smile.

The old woman left the store with her tea, tapping her cane in the snow, coughing away as she went. Lukas watched her through the window. She wore death like a coat, yet walked with serene determination, step by careful step across the square, with her burlap sack of flowers.

The clerk said he knew a man who might want to buy their horse. He could take them to him if they wished. Ona agreed, so the youth bundled into a fur and locked up his shop.

He led the children with the colt a short way out of the village, down a lane lined with birches, their branches laden with snow. They soon came to a farm. Here the land stretched out to the horizon, completely flat, blanketed in a sinister stillness. The small wood-beam house and barn were set away from the lane, surrounded by knobby apple trees holding out their arms in bewilderment. Their guide walked up to the door and knocked. Inside a dog barked with alarm. The door opened and a man appeared in the shadows of the house.

He was an enormous creature, this man, stouter than any they'd ever seen. The children waited mutely as the clerk explained to this giant what they wanted. The man retreated into the gloom of the house to don a coat and boots, and then emerged into the dusky yard to examine the horse.

In the window, Ona saw the face of a girl not much younger than her gazing forlornly through the pane at the strange travelers in the yard. Why did she appear so heartsick, Ona wondered? It was as if she were being held captive against her will in this giant's house. Ona would never see the girl again, yet in the months to come she would now and then think of her being stranded on this farm. In this way, the menace of the world would make itself known to Ona, in furtive glances and conjectures. Evil could be quiet and hidden, something almost unnoticed, yet it pricked the conscience all the same. The two girls' eyes met, and some private understanding seemed to pass between them.

Meanwhile, the big man was examining Chocolate with fastidious care, inspecting his teeth and hooves and flanks. In time, He finally announced that he would take the colt. He needed him for his plowing in the spring—his old horse of many years had just died last week. But he did not have any money with him now. He could pay them nothing.

—But we can't take nothing, said Ona.

The giant smiled, showing brown teeth.

—How much do you need, little girl?

When she told him eighty, he shook his head and spat.

—You think I am a fool?

—No sir.

—I will give you fifty.

—Seventy-five.

The man glowered at her, but then went inside the house. When he came out again, he had bills in his hand. He handed them to Ona; she counted sixty marks.

—It's not enough!

The giant laughed.

—It's all I have. Take it or leave it!

She didn't trust him, but it seemed they had no choice. She pocketed the cash, and the children said goodbye to the colt.

Back in the village, the clerk showed them to the train station, which was not really a station at all, but a hut with a ticket agent sitting behind a desk, awaiting passengers. They bought their tickets to Hamburg, which to their relief cost a fraction of what the giant had paid them, and then went to wait for the next train, due to arrive in two hours' time.

The tracks stretched eastward into Russia, westward into Prussia. Across the border, two guards patrolled in the red uniforms of the Czar. Aside from their pacing, all was still. A half-moon floated in the sky above. They hopped up and down in their boots to stay warm, though the cold began to gnaw at their toes. Soon they heard footsteps on the platform behind them: a woman in colorful skirts showing beneath her coat. She had large brown eyes that glittered in the gloom as she smiled at the children, who glanced quickly away. All their lives they'd been told to avoid looking these beggars in the eyes; they could curse you if you did, though what such a curse would mean was never explained.

Now the woman came up before them and spoke in accented Russian.

—Little ones, are you lost?

Ona dared to look up at the woman.

—We're waiting for the train.

—Give me money for something to eat.

Lukas looked at the woman. She reached out to touch his cheek, but he pulled away.

—We haven't any money, said Ona.

—It's a sin to lie.

—No money to spare.

—Everyone has money to spare for a hungry old woman.

She didn't look old, but Ona felt guilty all the same as she clutched the bills in her pocket.

—Leave us alone, she pleaded.

The woman saw their heavy satchels.

—You are going to travel across the ocean, she told them. You think I don't know you have money? You think I don't know you are holding your money tight in your hand?

She held out a palm. It looked worn and dirty and cold.

Ona glanced at her brother, who shook his head, but she slowly removed the precious wad of bills from her pocket. She unrolled the smallest bill she had and gave it to the woman.

—You see. You are already rich. You can spare more.

Ona shook her head vigorously, fearing she'd already given too much.

The woman began to leave, eying the girl darkly, murmuring as she went,

—There is more hunger in the world than you can possibly imagine.

Ona believed it. She watched the woman walk off, wondering if she'd done the right thing.

—You shouldn't have, said Lukas.

—She needed it.
—We do too!
—We'll have enough, she said, she hoped.
 A few minutes more, and the locomotive came screaming through the trees to the east. It raced over the rails, heavily slowing, the bulk of it chuffing out smoke, and the wheels wailed as the wide black face of the engine bore down.

A din of language filled the car—Yiddish, Polish, Russian, Lithuanian. Nearly every seat was taken, and luggage filled the racks above, so Ona and Lukas sat with their packs on their laps and watched in mute astonishment as a great discussion transpired among a Jewish family nearby. It had something to do with an apple. A white-bearded man in spectacles, held up the small, bruised apple, speaking to it as it were a person, until the others in the family laughed at whatever he'd said; then the man bit into the fruit, spraying juice into his beard. As he chewed, he glared at Ona; she looked away, embarrassed to have been caught looking. She stared up at the ceiling as the train car rocked and the fields flashed by the windows.
 The speed made Lukas smile, but Ona nervous. Neither one had been on a train before. Accelerating, they sat up

straight, holding onto their packs, as if the train might buck off the rails at any moment. But they only coasted over the flat land, and the people calmly carried on with their talk, as if all that secret murmuring in the dark car were propelling them forward.

Ona wanted to stay alert, to be on guard against thieves on this crowded train, but the rhythm of the rails kept lulling her to sleep, or almost asleep—she was conscious enough to feel the pressure of a body squeezing into the seat beside her—a boy, maybe a year or two older than her. He was strikingly thin and had the pale complexion of the malnourished. He looked straight ahead with large, solemn eyes, holding his own pack tightly on his lap, just as Ona and Lukas were doing with theirs. Was he, too, going to America? She was shy to ask. She was not used to strangers, had not been around so many before now, and it occurred to her that where she was going, there would be nothing but strangers—everywhere the eye looked, faces never before seen.

In four hours, they reached the edge of Danzig. The moon swung over the steeples, and all along the streets, lamps blazed. The children craned their heads to get a better look out the windows. They saw a broad avenue with people in hats walking by, trolley cars, horse-drawn carts, a distant glimpse of the sea, and the stony backs of buildings taller than anything in their village. In time, with great plumes of smoke and squealing wheels, the train rolled into the station and the doors opened.

Commotion filled the car as some passengers disembarked and others boarded. The children waited in suspense, gripping their bags, trying not to stare too long in anyone's eyes. Outside, on the platform, an old grandmother was making the sign of the cross over the heads of a younger woman, her three children, and husband, and all their eyes sparkled with tears. A handsome young woman was hugging her man goodbye, both finely dressed for the occasion of parting. A father on the platform bellowed last advice for two sons through the train windows. They nodded and laughed.

More and more people filed into their car, with all their satchels, baskets, and trunks, their tears and odors and warmth. Outside a man in a uniform and cap hollered, waved, blew his whistle, and the train doors clanked shut. The car lurched forward. The wheels groaned, shouts of parting erupted from the platform, and the people waved.

In the fields west of Danzig, Lukas opened his bag and found their mother's atlas. He unsnapped the clasp and opened its pages, which smelled of chamomile and caraway. It was too dark to read in the train, but he slipped his finger inside one of the envelopes and found dried lavender. He pulled out a leaf and ate it. His sister, watching, leaned over and kissed his head, as his mother might have done.

—We'll go back some day, she whispered.

But the train was carrying them so forcefully and swiftly westward, she doubted they would.

XIV

All along the dark hall sat patients waiting to see the doctor. They coughed and moaned and dozed in rickety wooden chairs. Karolina collapsed with relief into one of the chairs near the front door and leaned her head against the mahogany paneling. The air in the hall smelled of unwashed bodies, dank and cloying. Beside her, a woman nursed an infant hidden in thick folds of blankets. The creature made an eager suck-suck sound, and its legs churned under the grey cloth. The mother looked no older than seventeen. Her face was speckled all over with welts.

Years ago, when Ona had been a newborn, Karolina, too, had fallen ill; she'd never felt so sick, yet the baby required food and sought her breast night and day. Karolina had felt confused with resentment for her child, who demanded too much and was bursting with fresh vitality. It was as if all the mother's strength and good health had been used up to create the new life, and now the baby would have its revenge. She'd despised such thoughts, but had thought them all the same, and she remembered them now, looking at the sick mother's speckled face. Her eyes met Karolina's—a hard penetrating glare.

—How long have you been waiting? Karolina asked in Polish.

The woman shrugged as if to say time was of no account.

—Thirty minutes.
—How old?
—Three months.

Karolina nodded.

—A boy, the young mother volunteered.

Just then a door at the far end of the hall swung open, and a short round man in a dark suit stepped out, officiously making way for a man on crutches to limp into the hall.

—Next! the little doctor shouted.

An elderly woman with no teeth in her mouth rose

up and strode triumphantly toward the doctor, who had already disappeared into his office. All the people waiting shifted one seat closer to his door. Every ten minutes or so, a new patient would be called in, and they would all move forward. Despite the commotion, the baby fell asleep. The mother uncovered his head so that Karolina could see his little red face, the soft fuzz of blonde hair on his scalp, and his miniature hand curled in a hot ball pressed into the mother's breast—as Lukas had once done to her, just like that, his little fist grasping, his mouth sucking, the warmth spreading through her core. It all came back to her now, a rejuvenation, a swoon. Her children were still hers, she wanted them desperately. The infant stirred, turned his face into the mother' breast so Karolina could no longer see his features. Soon it was the girl's turn to go in.

Karolina would be next. She rose, moved to the chair next to the door. Behind her, a line stretched to the front of the townhouse. Did this stream of people ever cease? Did they line up every day, so many sick Poles? It was a wonder the city functioned with all this illness in the air, and so little to stop it from spreading. A man behind her launched into a rasping cough; the fit overtook him; he leaned over and coughed violently into his hands.

Karolina felt a tightness in her own chest as if his illness had already leaped into her lungs. Maybe it had been a mistake to stop here. She remembered now she had only a dime to give the doctor.

Before she could make up her mind to leave, the door opened once more; the mother walked out with her baby. She was clutching a bottle of something in her hand.

"Next!" came the doctor's voice from inside the office. Karolina rose to her feet.

The first thing she saw entering his office was a skeleton in the corner by the window. The yellowed skull leered at her.

—Five cents, please.

It was as if the bones had spoken, though the voice belonged to the doctor, Sadowski, who was no skeleton at all and pillowed with fat. He had thick, bushy black hair; his wiry goatee and mustache looked dusty and unfriendly. He was pointing to a tin money box on his desk.

—I only have a dime.

He opened the box and fished out a nickel. They traded coins.

—My cousin is ill, Karolina explained. Her fever is high and won't break, it keeps going up. Three days and she's worse than ever. I bought chamomile to make her tea, but I'm worried it won't be enough. Couldn't you come see her?

He opened a drawer in his desk, took out a vial of something, and handed it to her. At the touch of her palm, he took hold of it, felt its temperature, reached up to feel her cheek and forehead.

—Mother of God, what are you doing out? Go to bed as soon as you can. Give the syrup to your cousin in tea as often as she'll take it but save some for yourself. You'll both need it.

—Won't you come help her?

—You can see I'm busy.

—I'm afraid she's dying!

—As are we all, my dear.

He gave a wave of dismissal, turning his back to her. Karolina waited, wanting some saving word that would help her through the crisis. But he said nothing more. Turning at last to go, she opened her hand and looked at what he'd given her: it was elderberry syrup.

Outside again, she stood on the high stoop and placed the vial into the burlap sack with the chamomile flowers and honey. Her errands complete, it was time to return.

Snow had begun to fall again, the sky had dimmed, and the walkway filled with people heading home for the evening. She stood in a daze, feeling the flakes melting on her hot cheeks.

Where was she again? How to get home? But there was no home to return to, not here in this dreadful, beautiful, unfathomable city of strangers. She watched the people go by, longing for the warmth of home, for her Lukas and Ona...who were where just now? Doing what?

Step by step, she told herself, setting foot on Mulberry, turning north. She'd made a mistake coming all this way; she needed rest above all, and warmth. Step by step—each one an effort. She wished the man with the pocket watch would return to her side, lend her support, his mysterious strength. Who had he been? Why had he followed her all day long? Had she truly seen him at all?

It occurred to her that all the people passing her by on Mulberry, with their heavy coats and sturdy shoes leaving prints on the wet walkways—these people, too, were phantoms who'd soon be hidden in graves, even as new life spilled through these streets—new, nameless, procreating life: children clamoring for sustenance, mothers pushing apple carts, fathers pulling wagons heaped with coal and ash.

Here came one such wagon now: the black coal gleamed, dusted with snow. Breath fogged from the horse's wide nostrils; its feet clopped on the cobbles. Behind the beast sat a proud little man with red whiskers. He saw her watching him, and with a hand begrimed with coal, lifted his hat in a gallant gesture of greeting, then passed her by, never to be seen again.

She'd not yet grown accustomed to the speed of these faces coming and going. It seemed incomprehensible that they could pass her by, astonish her, and then disappear as if they'd never existed at all. She saw a steeple ahead—it would be a relief to enter once more into the comforting darkness of a church, but she'd dallied too long. She walked right by, turning to see in the church's doorway, a beggar huddled under a blanket. He had wild eyes that stared at nothing and everything. His hair was kinked in all directions. He was shivering, shivering, his lips looked blue, his face a ghastly pale. Down to her last nickel, she threw it to him, wondering how he endured the long winter nights.

She came once more to Houston, turned east. A gust of wind nearly knocked her over into some buckets of dried mushrooms an old woman was selling. If Karolina had had any money, she would've stopped to buy some. On a clear morning after a rain, she'd loved to venture into the wet woods near their village to gather chanterelles. She would go alone—as alone as she was now—and wander, her eyes on the moss, and the forest would speak to her. She'd come home in a trance, happy, her basket full. The children would be worried she'd been lost. *But I did get lost,* she'd tell them, *I always get lost in the woods—it's the only way to find the mushrooms.*

Now she walked by the woman, staring straight ahead at the back of a man with a limp. He moved as slowly as she did, and as carefully—each step an effort. As the wind picked up, his hat went sailing off his head, exposing tufts of gray hair. He glanced at the hat tumbling over Houston, under the feet of horses—they trampled it into some dung—then he kept on walking, throwing up his hands to heaven.

She was almost home now. Here was a newspaper merchant taking coins from a customer. What news of the world could possibly matter now? What a lot of inky nonsense, the news! Step by step, down Houston, past the knishery, its windows fogged with steam—she looked across the way to see if the man with the pocket watch might still be there, watching again, waiting to catch her if she fell.

Karolina turned the corner onto her shadowed, snowbound street, then paused to rest against a building. No matter the layers cloaking her body, she'd never felt so cold.

Ahead, on the stoop of the building across the street from her own, sat two figures. She recognized them or thought she did. These were the boys she'd seen from her window that morning—so many hours and blocks ago. She'd watched them choose whether to go left toward one fate or right toward another. Well, they'd gone left, and so? What had befallen them? They looked like statues in the cold.

As she pushed off from the building and walked toward the boys, a rat sidled across her path. It must have been slowed by the cold, for she nearly kicked it with her swinging black boot. The day coming to an end, rats prowled brave and free in the streets. A tattered wind blew paper scraps through the air, carrying the scent of a distant harbor with its briny hulls. Karolina thought of the ocean, its stormy darkness and depth. Why had she crossed it? Though she was not prone to regret, the question haunted her, as she crossed the snowy street to the front door of her building.

Before going in, she turned to look at the children. They were watching her with impassive white faces, unreadable, as much in this city was: the Yiddish newspapers, the knishery menu, the man with his watch, the woman in mourning...illegibility everywhere scrawled over the surface of the city in so much human script. Now, here, two more watchers watched with grave fascination as if her appearance were a sign of trouble. She turned away, opened the door, and went inside.

A damp warmth filled the stairwell. It smelled of boiled potatoes and onions, for it was that time of evening the women began to cook. Karolina climbed, pausing after every few steps to steady her throbbing head. Slowly, she ascended, hearing the encouraging sounds of home around her, of infants crying, mothers scolding, little feet running down halls.

On the third-floor landing, an old man sat smoking his pipe, as he often did come evening. His wife must have disapproved of the smoke and so made him take the business out here, with a little glass jar for ashes beside the rickety packing crate on which he sat. The smoke wreathed round his bald head was thick and delicious. It reminded Karolina of someone from back home—someone very close to her and important had smoked a pipe, too, but who had it been? The past rose up in a blur of indistinct color and emotion. Why couldn't she make out her father's face? She knew it was her father, yet he remained hidden in a fog. On the landing, she wobbled on her boots and nearly fell into the man's lap but saved herself by slumping against the wall. He spoke a few delicate words in a language that sounded nothing like Polish or Russian or any tongue she knew. Seeing that she did not understand, he muttered a few words in English with a puff of pipe smoke:

—Boats two cents any color.

Karolina shut her eyes and tried to decode the meaning of this man's fragrant utterance. He spoke again:

—Boats two cents any color. *Boats* two cents any color.

She translated the words in her mind backward and forward before she grasped some hint of promise in the phrase; perhaps it was a sales mantra he'd memorized and repeated on a street corner. The phrase now served, when all other language failed, as his badge of identity. She nodded, and he smiled at her so benevolently that she reached out with her trembling hand and touched him on the cheek.

As she walked up the last flight of stairs, she heard him mutter his truth once more:

—Boats two cents any color!

She heard commotion behind the black door. She hoped, unreasonably, to find her cousin Marija restored to health, at work in the kitchen, perhaps preparing a batch of curd dumplings. She would be bending over the table in the center of the room, smoothing out a sheet of dough with a rolling pin, a blush on her cheek, blonde tresses spilling, and the sun, though it had set by now, would nevertheless be shining through the grimy window. A fantasy, Karolina knew, as she took out her key and opened the door.

There in the kitchen sat the bereaved Polish mother from the back room. Still dressed in black, small and pale, she ate from a bowl of buckwheat gruel. Karolina wondered where the men of the family were at this hour. Out drinking? Drowning grief the easy way, leaving this mother alone with her catastrophe? The infant had died just two weeks ago. Since then, the mother had scarcely left her room to cook or eat, but here she was, her face stripped bare by pain. A single candle flickered on the table, showing her eyes to be red and swollen.

She said nothing to Karolina, who went straight to the stove to put on a kettle for tea. It was warm in the flat, compared to outside, but Karolina still felt cold in her bones so left on her coat. She took two tin mugs down from a shelf—one for her, one for Marija.

The mother had been watching.

—You've got it, she announced in Polish.

—What?

—You've got the grippe—I see it in your eyes.

Her son emerged from the back room. A fair-haired, mal-nourished creature, he seemed to live in the shadows. He'd not spoken to Karolina once, but he stared at her now.

—Stay away from her! the mother commanded, and the child at once retreated into the room where he lived and worked, sewing hems on garments for his mother. She got up herself, took her bowl of gruel into the next room, and slammed the door shut against any contagions that might float their way.

Karolina went into the bedroom to check on Marija. She was in the same spot where she'd been this morning. She was still sleeping, only she'd pushed her blankets to the side and had unbuttoned her gown to expose her throat and upper chest, which was damp with perspiration. Her hair, too, was wet, and her cheeks had flushed crimson, as her eyes roved about with restless dreaming behind half-closed lids. She looked beautiful to Karolina, as sick as she was; the fever had broken.

She went quietly back to the kitchen to sit and wait for the water to boil. As she shut her eyes, the building seemed to be adrift on some inner sea, dark and vast. Her breath was growing short. The effort it took simply to breathe made her want to cry. The kettle was creeping toward its boil. Had she forgotten something? The lemons, yes, and her children, too—left behind on the other side of the earth. The kettle shrieked its accusation.

She concocted the tea with the brittle chamomile flowers, which smelled fragrant and sunny, like home. The elderberry syrup came out thick, nearly black with sweetness. Finally, the honey dripped from her spoon into the mugs, and she poured the steaming water over it all.

Karolina carried this potion to the bedroom she shared with her cousin. She shut the door with her boot and carefully placed the cups on a nightstand between their two cots. It was nearly dark in the room. At last, Karolina undid the clasps of her coat, removed it with a terrible inward shiver. She rapidly stripped her sick body bare, threw on a nightgown, and flung herself under the quilts. At once, she began to weep—with guilt for all her mistakes, her foolish journeying about the world. For a time, she forgot about the steaming tea on the nightstand, for which she'd travelled so far. Having laid her head down, she knew at once it was too heavy to lift again.

She thought of the man in the stairwell: *boats two cents any color.* The refrain played in her head. She wished he would think to climb the flight of stairs and come to her side, to take care of her, for Karolina wanted badly now to be cared for by someone. A senile old man from a faraway land would do. He'd reminded her of her father; his pipe smoke had. She traveled a long way back now, to the sight of her dead father in the woods, adding one more mushroom to the others in the basket he carried. He looked small among the pines; he looked almost gone in the shadows; but he was there, gathering food for the family, and Karolina was with him, her feet in the moss. It was terribly good to be home.

The sleep began to pull on her, and the tea cooled, and the light of the sun went out over Manhattan in the year 1901.

XV

Ona slept long on the train as it rumbled through Polish towns and fields. When she awoke, she didn't know where she was, only that she was accelerating through darkness, and it was cold. She reached into her pocket to ensure the bills were still there. They were, but her brother was gone.

A man in the door of the train car stood idly watching her. His face looked pale and narrow; a thin black mustache twitched over his mouth. She could get up to find Lukas, but to do so she'd have to leave the bags behind, and she didn't want the man to take them. So, she stayed put, trying to make out the shapes flashing dimly by in the night—barns, silos, windmills.

Snowflakes splattered against the pane and slid wildly over the glass.

The man in the door came into their compartment and sat in the seat opposite hers. He smiled, then spoke to her in a language she did not understand. His gaze seemed to reach inside her and demand something she could not give.

He spoke again, more decisively, yet quietly enough not to wake the passengers sleeping all around them. Then he reached over to touch her knee. He massaged it, smiling. She held her breath, unable to move.

The car rocked along the rails. It was so dark she could only see the glint of his eyes and the pale sheen of his oily face. She heard him speak three senseless words, like a magical incantation. His hand began to reach under the hem of her dress. It grasped her bare knee. He reached higher up her thigh with rough fingers.

Just then her brother returned. He stopped in the car door, meeting her panicked gaze. Without a thought, he threw his body onto the stranger's neck. He squeezed with both arms, yanking him backwards. The intruder jumped to his feet, threw off the boy, and hurried out of the car. A few nearby passengers woke to see what had happened, but the trouble had so quickly passed that they gradually settled back down and closed their eyes. The children stared at each other.

—Where *were* you?

—Walking. Up the train and back. What did he do?

Beginning to cry, she stared at the window, at the wet snow streaking across the glass. Lukas came to sit beside her.

The man was gone, but the train was small; he could easily return.

—What did he do? he whispered again.

She didn't answer. Nothing like that had happened to her before, though she'd been warned it someday would. Her mother had told her, when Ona turned fourteen, that men would begin to reach for her—first with their eyes, then with their hands—and that she must not let them touch, must do what she needed to stay safe—run, scream, bite, claw. Her mother had told her these things in a whisper, one night in Ona's bed, holding her hand, telling her she would have to be strong and fierce in her absence, for she was about to leave for America. Her mother had tears in her eyes, a sight so extraordinary to Ona that she promised at once, of course, she would be strong and fierce. But Ona had been neither. That man had touched her without hesitation, as if he'd had every right, and he'd known she'd let him. She hadn't fought back, hadn't even called for help. She would have sat there as he'd reached and groped and done what he'd wanted.

Would the cities of the world be filled with such beastly men? Would such things happen as a matter of course? Her heart raced with the train over the frozen fields. For hours, she would have to stay alert. She opened her eyes wide, bit her lip, watched the car door, and every time it opened and a conductor or passenger came through, she flinched. But the tall thin man with the mustache did not return.

They watched the light come in. It spread wide and pale over snow-blanketed farms. Passengers began to wake. The train stopped now and then to let in new passengers with crates and luggage for their journey across the ocean. Rich-looking families—women in fine hats and dresses, men in their best suits—came through the car issuing orders to obedient children. They didn't even look at Ona and Lukas, just two more faces among the crowds, which would grow bigger, more complex, and various the further west they traveled.

In time, they came into the outskirts of a city. A blur of warehouses, sheds, and alleys rushed by. Voices in the train rose with excitement. They raced through a dark tunnel, burst into bright sun, and gulls whirled over distant steeples as the train slowed its great bulk. They passed crowded streets, messy with people and wagons, and the light looked so fresh, so clean and newly made for the day that the children felt instinctively hopeful.

Soon they were disembarking with all the others onto a crowded platform. They spotted the mustached man at once—he stalked up ahead, tall and gangly, a small crate on his bent back. At least Ona thought it was him. She couldn't be sure; it had been so dark. He was walking in the opposite direction so that he passed the children, and his gaze met Ona's. He smiled in recognition, a look that chilled her to her core. She turned away and gathered her satchels.

—Let's go, she said.

The port couldn't be so hard to find. All they would have to do was follow the people, and they did so, into the main terminal, where, beneath a ticking clock, they came upon a smelly clown juggling teacups. He'd placed a soiled hat on the floor for spare change. Not knowing which way to go, they paused for a time to watch the juggler. The three teacups rose and fell in a high arc over the clown's head. He had long, lanky blonde hair and a face painted white with a red frown smeared thickly over his lips. He stared forlornly into the distance and did not appear to notice the children's presence; nor did he seem to attend to the cups, which fell into his hands as if attached to them by invisible string. A faded carnation hung limply out of the buttonhole of his jacket. Lukas looked into the hat on the ground and saw only a few copper coins. He still had a few coins left over from the rubles he'd stolen from his uncle back home. He dropped these into the hat; they were Russian and worthless, but the clown didn't know, and gave a little smile, though the painted frown kept on frowning all the same.

—Lukas, let's go. We can't just stand here, said Ona, trying to pull him toward the doors leading into the street. Her brother didn't want to leave; he'd never seen such a sight, not once in his years had he seen a juggler. He had the urge to sit himself down beside the clown and draw him in his notebook. And so, he yanked his arm free from his sister's grasp and opened his bag, found his paper and pencil, and settled down on the floor to sketch. He noticed how the makeup was smeared around the man's eyes and lips, and the droplets of sweat at his temple. When a little audience gathered, the clown began to sing a ballad as he kept on juggling, and when it came to an end, the people clapped politely. A woman dropped several coins into the clown's hat, and so did an old gentleman, and the clown nodded ever so slightly as he went on juggling. Soon they all left him, but the boy kept sketching, filling in more detail around his eyes. A clock above chimed the hour, causing a pigeon to flutter overhead, trapped, like this clown, inside the Hamburg terminal.

Soon Ona would drag the boy from the station, but not before he left his sketch in the clown's hat as a gift.

Neither Ona nor Lukas would notice that their mother's book of remedies had fallen out of his satchel onto the floor of the terminal. The clown would not notice either, busy as he was examining the boy's sketch as the children walked off into the city.

The street streamed with life, with wagons and walkers, with police on stallions and black hansoms rattling over wet cobbles. Buildings taller than oaks towered on either side, casting long shadows over pedestrians below. Who were they to follow? The people were going in all directions; there was no clear path, no obvious way to turn, but a sudden push toward the right swayed the children to go that way, too, and so they did, trying to match the pace, which was swift and serious.

They soon passed a bakery with its doors propped open. The scent of warm bread gusted over their heads, and their little stomachs cried out. But a line of men in black coats inside the shop intimidated the children into moving on. They came to an intersection where the crowd dispersed and carts pulled by horses clogged the way as people streamed around them, high-stepping over horseshit in the road. As the children picked their way around a cart full of coal, Lukas had the uncanny sensation that he'd been here before, in this very place, walking around a coal wagon, in a sun-drenched city of strangers—an impossible fantasy, a trick of the mind, surely, yet it struck him as so indelible and true an impression that he stopped to ponder it and look all around him for a sign of familiarity.

Just then a throng of bearded men in black hats came walking in the opposite direction, rushing by him as Ona pushed on. Then the cart moved, and all the city kept moving, and Lukas, try as he might, could not regain the conviction that had filled him with such certainty. By the time he snapped out of his reverie and resumed walking, he could no longer see his sister. He could see nothing but a thicket of strangers in coats hustling this way and that.

He began to run, calling her name. He stumbled on an icy curb and nearly fell against a wide-hipped woman. Thinking him a pickpocket, she swiped at the boy, knocked him smartly on the crown. He ran off, sprinting back the way they had come.

Discovering her brother's absence, Ona stopped in her tracks. She turned back, retraced her steps to the intersection where they seemed to have parted ways. To the left, the twin belfries of a church rose above a narrow street. That Lukas might have headed toward the church seemed plausible enough, so she hurried toward it, shyly calling his name, hearing nothing in reply but the murmur of Germans going about their errands.

She might well have lost him forever. In a city so vast, with so many streets twined together, and so many humans clogging them all, two souls could wander in search of each other for the rest of their lives and never once cross paths. She hurried all the way to the church front and stood gawking at the powerful belfries as one began to ring out. Great, echoing shudders of sound passed through her bowels as she stood there. Behind her, a street curved away into shadows.

She headed slowly back toward the station. She heard a squeal not unlike her brother's laugh, but it was only a rusty wagon wheel on a brougham rolling by. She called his name weakly into the street. No one answered but a gull diving for a breadcrumb with a wild flap of wings. It swooped and swallowed its prize, and people kept walking by, not one of them a boy; her brother was not here. She hollered his name, and a round little woman came up to her side to say something brusque, to which Ona could make no reply, so fearful was she that she'd done something unforgivably wrong in losing her brother.

Then the crowds parted, and she saw the bakery and Lukas standing by its door. Their eyes met, and they ran toward each other like long-lost lovers.

She wept. He blushed. She scolded him. How dare he leave her! How dare he run off! They might have been lost forever! He began to cry.

—Oh, stop it, she told him. What we need is food. Let's get some bread.

They bought a fat loaf and devoured it right there in the bakery, in silence, tearing into the crust with their teeth. When they'd eaten one loaf, they bought another and ate that, too. Then, in his notebook, Lukas quickly drew a ship next to a question mark and showed it to the girl behind the counter.

She didn't understand at first, but then she noticed their scuffed, travel-weary satchels and understood they sought the port. She drew them a crude map in the child's notebook, writing the names of the streets they were to follow, in a list, with little arrows directing them to turn right or left. She told them how to go, in German, gesturing with her hands, smiling and laughing at the uncomprehending children, as if this were a delightful game they were playing. She set them off, thoroughly confused by her directions and map.

What was a city but a maze with no center, searching for its own impossible solution? So it seemed to Lukas and Ona as they began to navigate their way toward the port. They progressed slowly, looking out for street signs at every turn. People rushing by seemed impatient with the children's slowness. Whenever the boy saw a policeman, a jolt of adrenaline shot through him, for he sensed he could be arrested at any moment, simply for being where he did not belong.

He clutched his sister's hand as they made their way deeper into the city.

Soon it became clear where to go. The city spilled into the port. Many roads led there, and so did the crowds—travelers with trunks and luggage, with wicker baskets full of linen and heirlooms. They could tell they were approaching the water from the racket of gulls overhead, and the people began to walk faster, as if pushed along by an invisible hand, a spirit telling them to hurry, hurry, space might be running out. And everyone obeyed this spirit, this dark angel, and rushed along the narrow streets, as the gulls spiraled above.

They came at last to an expanse of glassy water cluttered with ships and boats. Along the docks on either side, people gathered in confused clumps. One crowd had amassed near a ship that towered over all the others on the water. The children had never seen anything so large. It was bigger, by far, than their village church. Its massive hull, resting lightly on the water's edge, looked as if it contained a vast and secret world. Seeing the ship, Lukas wanted badly to board it, to run through its hidden rooms. The desire was adulterated by fear, too, of the open sea, which he had never seen, and of the secretive ship itself, which looked at once heavy and light. But he took courage from the crowd gathered on the dock. If all these travelers were so eager to board, if the masses saw fit to travel thus across the charted seas, as so many had already done, then Lukas and Ona, too, could embark. Perhaps, he thought, casting his eye toward the far reaches of the harbor, the Atlantic was not so large as he'd imagined. Word was it took only a week to reach the other side.

They walked toward the water and soon saw a sign on a stone building that read HAMBURG-AMERIKA.

—*There*, said Ona, squeezing the money in her pocket.

A crowd was forming at the doors of the building, and the children joined it, waiting their turn to enter. A din of language in the briny air confused them until, like a bell, they heard the sound of their mother tongue behind them. Trying to seem inconspicuous, they turned to see a young mother not much older than Ona holding a baby in her arms, and a man in his twenties loaded with suitcases, sweat streaking from his temples. They were talking about the baby, who was screaming. The mother said he was hungry and needed to nurse; the father said he would have to wait, the line was moving. Indeed, they were all shuffling forward with the crowd. Ona shouted over the noise, in their own language,

—Is this where we can pay for the passage?

The parents looked shocked to hear their tongue spoken so far from home. But then the man simply nodded, and said,

—It is.

They moved forward once again into the dark hall, where the line snaked around in tight coils before dividing into queues leading to six ticket windows. The baby began to scream. The mother unbuttoned her blouse and pressed his soft head to her breast. He began to nurse, his little limbs twitching beneath his blankets.

—Are you going to America?

The woman nodded.

—Today?

The man said the ship would leave tomorrow. They'd be staying in a pension for the night.

The line moved slowly forward. The murmur in the hall sounded tense—a dull roar on the verge of becoming a shriek. The tension had to do with money. The children could see men at the ticket windows counting out heaps of bills for the agents. Ona worried they wouldn't have enough, and if they didn't, what then? What could they sell? They had nothing anyone would care to buy.

After nearly an hour of waiting, they came to the window and faced an agent in spectacles that glinted with electric light. He said what sounded like hello to the children and pointed to the bottom of a column of numbers on a sign behind him. Ona took out her bills and began to count out the money, which felt now insubstantial and cheap in her hands; she could not believe they could exchange it for anything at all, but the agent scooped up the bills she presented and handed her back some coins. He began to write on a pad of paper.

He barked a single word at the children, but they did not understand him. He barked the word again and again, and they simply stared, holding onto the counter with both hands. Then the agent called for a colleague to come, and another uniformed man arrived in the window. He looked almost exactly like the first, with glinting spectacles, but he spoke to the children in Russian.

—Show us your names, surnames, and ages— hurry now!

They had brought with them their baptismal certificates from the village church. These papers, tattered and worn from handling, covered in Cyrillic lettering, were the only documents on the earth that testified to their identities. Ona opened her satchel, fumbling with the latches, and dug inside to find the certificates, which she'd folded many times and hidden inside a sock. She felt ashamed of the musty, grey wool sock she took out before the eyes of these agents, who could refuse to sell them passage if they so wished. But when she took out the certificates and unfolded them, the first agent grabbed the papers. Seeing them, he shouted in frustration, for the writing was in Russian and he couldn't understand a word. But the second agent helped to translate, as his colleague wrote down their names and ages on the pad of paper. He tore off the top page and slid it across to the children.

—This is your contract for passage, said the second agent. Be careful not to lose it.

At the top of the contract, in bold black letters, were the words *Hamburg Amerika Linie, Hamburg*. Beneath were blocks of German text and a place where their names and ages had been scrawled in black ink.

—When does the ship leave? Ona asked the agent in Russian.

—Tomorrow morning at ten. Don't be late.

They spent the night in a church near the harbor.

After buying their passage, they'd gone inside with the idea of lighting a candle. Lukas had suggested it as they were walking by the church entrance. He'd always been the more prayerful one—a stubborn believer, like their mother, in charms and blessings.

The interior of the church was surprisingly spacious, with a vaulted ceiling supported by heavy stone columns.

Dusty blue light angled through high windows onto pews below, where a few people sat or kneeled in silence, their breath fogging the air. In a corner chapel, the children found an array of votive candles before a statue of Mary. Ona wouldn't spare a cent, but Lukas lit a candle anyway, and they stood before it.

The boy thought of his mother's eyes. They were the holiest thing he knew on earth, but the longer he prayed on them, the more they wavered, like the candle's guttering flame. When he tried to make the image hold still, shadows fell over it, and he could hear nothing but doubts.

Beside him, his sister's thoughts floated out on the ruffled waters of an ocean she'd never seen. She imagined infinite depths and watery vacancy spreading in all directions. She sought solace in the thought of the map of the world she'd seen in the basement of the village church—a map on which the Atlantic's blue was a matter of inches, shallower than a teardrop, and could be spanned in a dream.

So the children prayed, and when they tired, they retreated to the pews in the side of the church. It was all dark and quiet, and no one seemed to have noticed their presence. It was not proper, surely, to lay yourself down in a pew, but they did so, and no one paid them any mind, not even when they fell fast asleep.

They didn't wake up before it was dark and the heavy doors closed. They sat up refreshed in the moonlit cavern among the columns of stone. They shivered as footsteps sounded from deep within the church, behind the altar. They heard a door open and slam shut, then no more footsteps.

The thought crossed both their minds: they'd slept through their ship's departure time. But this couldn't be, it was still night, they had hours yet to kill. In the silent church, they walked up to the front doors to discover that they'd been bolted shut with a key. There was no knowing when the doors would be unlocked again. They turned around and looked down the long aisle to the altar with its silver cross catching moonlight.

They walked down that aisle over slate stones, then behind the altar, to the sacristy in the back, where they found a side door, and this, too, had been bolted shut with a key they lacked. There was no sign of anyone they might ask for help, but when they came out to the main church, they found a black cat watching them with bright eyes from beneath a pew. It crept out, raised its back, and hissed, so they kept their distance, returning to where they'd slept. They sat there, tired, looking at the Mother of God with the infant in her arms.

—It's cold, said Lukas.

—Hug me.

—Okay.

—It helps? asked Ona.

—A little.

—What if they don't unlock the doors in time?

—We break a window and run for it.

—The windows are too high up.

—We'll pound on the doors, he said. We'll scream.

Soon they became too cold to sit still. Lukas suggested they run races down the center aisle of the church, and since no one was there to tell them it was wrong, they did just that. The brother and sister knelt in the back of the church near the front doors, on either side of a holy water well, and got ready to race, and then they ran, as hard as they could, down the long aisle, raucously laughing, for their footsteps were loud. Though her legs were longer, and though she was older, Ona let her quick little brother reach the altar railing first. They raced many times, and the boy usually won, until he got angry at his sister for losing on purpose. She won all the races after that, until Lukas suggested they make friends with the black cat.

They found it in the sacristy, curled up in some cassocks in a cabinet, dozing. They opened all the cabinets in that little room and also found a spare chalice, a loaf of stale bread, and a bottle of wine. They opened the wine and took turns drinking, smiling at each other with the wine on their lips. They liked how it made them feel, warm and loose, and they went giggling back into the church, talking about how much trouble they'd be in if the priest back home, who was terribly strict, could see them now. Of course, he couldn't, he was in Siberia, no one could see them at all except maybe God, and Jesus, and Mary, and whatever saints those were pictured in the stained-glass windows high above—so many faces were floating in that glass, so many pairs of eyes looking down on the children, who'd stolen from their uncle, stolen a horse, and now had guzzled the blood of Christ like water.

    The wine helped them sleep again, and they did not wake up until a pair of hands roughly grabbed hold of their coat collars and yanked them upright in the pew. A man was yelling at them, yelling words they couldn't understand, spittle flying off his purple mouth. The children grabbed their satchels and hustled out of the pews toward the church doors. The man, a priest in black, followed them out, yelling all the while, until the children pushed open the doors and escaped onto the steps, where they stood for a time, blinking in the sunlight, dazed, their heads still swimming with wine and strange dreams.

They soon made their way back to the great ship. They found it waiting at the dock, looming like a world in its nascency.

They would recall the ocean as nothing but a place of surrender. For once they boarded the ship, they no longer had choices of their own to make; they gave themselves up to the tremor and speed of the hulking craft. Feeling its power in their feet, they were at its mercy. With a festival of cheers from the crowded decks, the ship drifted out of the harbor, into the open sea, and set its course inexorably westward. Ona and Lukas huddled at the railing in the frigid air, gaping at the expanse of slate-gray water.

It would seem to have passed swiftly, their journey across the water, as if time itself, after leaving the Old World, had become untethered and obeyed new rules—machinery that cut through days like that steamer churned through waves.

In fact, the crossing took six days, five nights, and it was only on the third night of their journey, out on the deck, that Lukas would open his satchel and look for his mother's atlas. He would find it missing and begin to cry. Ona would try to console him, to no avail. He cried a long time and it was only the wind that calmed him—the wind that whipped the tears off his face—and the stars, plentiful and bright in the cold sky, which told him plainly that his childhood was a small, lost thing, and there could be no more tears in the brave days to come.

XVI

In the woods again—old growth pines, spindly birch, a forest floor sparkling with snow. Karolina walked through it, startling sparrows into the sky.

Where was she going? Deeper in. That was all that mattered. Trunks cast long blue shadows over the ground; she felt their cool breath. Her mother and father, long gone, were somewhere out here. She would reach them if she walked far enough. There were no more demands now—no more streets to follow or errands to run. New York had fallen away, sloughed into nothing. But this pine forest, this crusted snow, these footsteps and sparrows—all these were hers; she belonged here; her parents did; they, too, lived on in this dusk.

But it was terribly cold in the woods. She wanted warmth. She ran out of the pines into a meadow where all was sunlit, green, and flowering; soft grasses grew tall on the banks of the Merkys. Her old home was in the distance. Her children would be there.

A sense of waiting and dread fell upon the meadow, as if God's eyes had turned upon her to see what she would do. The flowers supplied an answer. She would gather herbs to keep Lukas and Ona well. She knew where to find the good plants—angelica, caraway, coltsfoot. She set out, wading through warm grasses; they swished against her skirts.

High in the sky, storks were circling and circling, preparing to fly south for the winter. It was late summer. The long cold nights would soon roll in.

She was dying: the fact wormed its way up from the murk of her body. And this is what death looked like—storks circling, like buzzards, only more festive, more marvelous, with white whirls and loops in the sky.

She stared long at the birds until the woman in mourning appeared with her black umbrella aloft. She held out a hand to Karolina, who accepted the help and soon found herself walking arm in arm down Broome Street, leaning on the stranger for support as they went.

—Where are we going?
—Home, of course.
—You don't even know where I'm from, said Karolina.
—But I do.

The woman led her down Broome to the banks of the Merkys, and there they began to gather chamomile. Bees murmured among the blossoms. Sunshine warmed her shoulders. When they had as much as their hands could carry, they walked away from the river, up the hill to the cemetery, and there set the flowers down on Karolina's grave.

—Not yet, she pleaded.
—Aren't you ready?
—We've forgotten Ona and Lukas.
—But they've gone, my darling.
—Gone?
—Looking for you.

Karolina backed away from the woman—slowly at first, but then she bolted like a deer, away from her own flower-strewn grave, and raced across a field. She came to a train station, which she recognized at once—it was where she'd said goodbye to her children. They were nowhere to be found now—not in the terminal, nor on the long barren platform. The only one present was an old man in a conductor's uniform sitting on a bench.

Where had her children gone, she asked him?

—Boats two cents any color, he said.

A train came groaning into the station. Karolina jumped on it, and so was carried off, inside a car full of laughing men.

Oh, this is an absurd sort of dream, she thought. She would have to find her children and tell them she was ill; she needed their help, she needed them soon—

—Why are you running off? said the woman in mourning, who was at her side again. Didn't you want to go home? Don't you remember the storks?

She took Karolina by the hand, but Karolina pulled herself free and jumped right off the moving train. She tumbled into a soft meadow, rolled down a slope to the riverbank, and sat up among the chamomile and the bees.

There was her son, naked as a fish, swimming in the river. She waded out, too, and held him up so he floated lightly on his back. The water sluiced around his head and shoulders. He smiled, with his eyes closed.

She'd done this before; this had happened, long ago, and now he was gone. Her arms were full of cold water flowing.

She shut her eyes, and the darkness spun in a dizzying

vortex. She was sinking, sinking—into the river. Her spirit relaxed. The current could take her. Why struggle against it?

On land, in slashing sunshine, her boy's legs ran along, chasing. But she let go at last and sank into a watery depth, landing gently on the sandy floor below.

Pine trees grew from the sand into the sky.

She sat up in the forest, stood, and began to walk.

Here is my story, she told herself. This small life of mine, these comings and goings, flights and distances—tracts so dense with trees you can't find your own name in them. She reached out for her name and could not recall it. She was an infant being baptized in a priest's rough arms. Her family waited in the pews, a kept secret. Her parents watched her be cleansed of what sin? What had she done or failed to do? No matter, the water washed over her; she was as faultless as a star.

They all stood outside in the cold watching the night sky. Christmas. Not long ago, her children watched at her side as a streak of light in the heavens made them shout. Such clean frozen winter stars! She wanted them back, wanted her children back. I'm dying, but the stars will shine on, and the children's lives will unspool into the world like thread, winding and snagging over fields without me.

She yearned herself out into the wind, let herself extend and rush zephyr-like over the sea...but the children were gone.

The fog came through the trees. It lingered over the moss. All was damp. Once again, she was gathering mushrooms in the forest—food for the dead—in a basket hanging on her arm. She was glad to find a chanterelle in the moss. She cut it free with her pocketknife and placed the fleshy protuberance into her basket.

She found another, then another. In the distance, among the trees, she saw children running. They were hers. Her heart clamored for them. She walked, then ran toward them, but they'd vanished into the trees. She tripped and fell, landing in a bed of moss. She rolled over onto her back and looked through the lattice of branches into the dusk sky. Snowflakes began to drift through the air onto her face, pinpricks of cold.

By her side, a wolf rested on its haunches. Its gray fur was ragged, its breath made soft clouds. The dying light of day shone on its eyes, which looked so gently upon Karolina that she was convinced: there was no more reason to fight or resist. She gazed into those eyes and saw herself as a sliver of fading light. There was nothing else in the world, only that glimmer in the wolf's bright eye—a glimmer that was her body. It guttered and flickered, and at last she gasped.

And so it was: with a streak in the night sky, she was a child again, watching her own death on a Christmas night. Oh, I died, I died, just like that—

Yet her children were calling.

XVII

The island was a crucible. Mute and fearful, the children queued in long lines to have their eyes, teeth, and bodies examined by rough-fingered men. A stench floated over the crowd that spilled through the cavernous building. Now and then, throughout the hours-long ordeal, the children caught glimpses out windows of a harbor's sheen, the streak of a gull, a distant boat adrift.

They'd been warned by fellow passengers on the ship they'd be sent back: they were too young to enter the country alone and must have been let on board by mistake. The prospect of return too terrible to countenance, they'd disbelieved the claims. All they would have to do was prove their mother awaited them. And so, before docking, in the last hours of the voyage, Lukas had sat on deck and drawn once more, in pencil, the face of his mother. He rendered her from memory, her solemn gray eyes and soft questioning mouth. He knew well the drawing was imperfect, yet owing to the speed with which he drew, the rendering possessed an urgency such that, when it was placed at last before the guard in the great hall, it held his attention. He might have pushed it aside, yelled at its author, demanded to see his real papers, but instead he looked—first at the face of the mother on the page, and then at the boy, who so closely resembled her. Perhaps he understood. Perhaps he saw the address that Ona had carefully written beneath the drawing—201 Henry Street, New York—and recognized what these lost children were trying to say. This spectacled man, harried by masses, ought to have demanded the boy and his sister be sent back, but in a moment of charity he only asked, in Russian, for their names, which they breathlessly provided. He wrote them down in a book, and then waived them through a gate.

On the ferry's deck, the children held each other's hands, their eyes directed at the buildings stacked high on the island's edge. Cold winds whipped over the harbor, against their backs, chopping up waves that splashed on the pilings. The city sent ribbons of smoke from countless chimneys into a grimy sky. From a distance, New York looked like an apparition, a fantasy penciled onto the gray canvas of the day. But as the ferry floated closer, details emerged – the black shadows of towers, carriages and horses, a flock of gulls, people crowding the dock, expectant, bustling, waving at the approaching vessel.

The children squeezed each other's hands, afraid to disembark. Yet when the ferry nestled against the dock, its passengers, heaving their luggage, began to shuffle ashore. The children had no choice but to join the queue and walk through an iron gate, into what appeared to be a park. Joyous shouts went up as those who'd arrived discovered loved ones in the commotion. Two men in long coats hugged tearfully in front of the children, who kept looking at the women in the crowd; they hoped against reason their mother might have intuited their arrival and so come down to this dock to greet them. Of course, each face they saw was entirely unlike their mother's. No one seemed to notice the children at all. No one called or waved or asked if they needed a ride in a taxi or offered to take their bags. It was as if they were invisible, walking through the crowd down a path that wound under some trees, past a cast-iron cannon, toward the hulking buildings of the city.

A stench of watery rot wafted off the harbor—dead fish in the swill. Exhausted, confused, uncertain where to go, the children stopped at a railing overlooking the waves. Gulls crossed the darkening sky. It was late afternoon.

—We have to find her before nightfall, said Ona in a whisper for fear that someone nearby might hear and insist upon their return.

Lukas took out his drawing and looked at the address beneath it.

—Henry Street, he said thickly, the words not at home in his mouth.

Mapless, they would have to ask for help—but whom to approach? Everyone here was on the move, hustling one direction or another with purpose. The children, too, wanted to join the flow, for it seemed dangerous to stand still and so make oneself conspicuous. They began to walk, hoisting their satchels over their shoulders, veering away from the crowd. Near the entrance to the park, they saw an old man on a bench. He was hugging himself as if trying to stay warm. Something in the way he was looking around the park made it seem that he, too, might be lost. Yet when his eyes fell upon the faces of the two children, it occurred to Ona that this man might tell them what they needed to know. And so, she stopped before him and only then noticed the dirt on his face, the bits of grass in his bushy white beard, and holes in his frayed coat. The smell that came off him warned her away, but it was too late—he was looking up with childish wonder at Ona, as if expecting her to present him with a gift. She took from her brother the drawing of their mother beneath which they'd written out her address. She presented the paper, pointing directly at the words *Henry Street*, and waited.

He looked down, muttering to himself; he squinted, pressed his face close to see better. Then he examined the children's faces and said something in a high, gravelly voice they could not understand. He seemed to repeat himself, pointing at the address, and then the drawing. He was asking a question. A third time he repeated himself, so loudly now it sounded as if he were angry. Ona's instinct was to grab the paper and run, but now he was smiling at them, smiling as if he knew something of value they did not. He handed it back, looked up at the sky, and finally pulled from a pocket in his coat an old watch with a cracked and splintered face. He checked the time and struggled to stand. He was not a tall man. His bare white head came no higher than Ona's nose. He began to walk out of the park. After several slow steps, he stopped, turned, and waved at Ona and Lukas to follow.

They obeyed, this man their only clue, their only foothold on the vast face of the city.

His pace was slow but unflagging. They followed him a few steps behind, into the shadows cast by the towers on either side of the narrow street. The children wanted to stare at the spectacle of these structures, to take in their stone immensities, but they did not dare risk losing the old man in the crowd.

Though after a block they began to wonder if he was aware that they were following him. He did not look back to confirm their presence as he crossed a street patched with dingy ice. He pressed on, and Ona wanted to know if they were headed north, south, east or west, though it would make no difference to her if she did know this, for she had no map of the island in her mind; she had never seen such a map, and Manhattan was far more massive than she'd imagined it to be. For all she knew, Henry Street could be just around the corner or a three days' journey from where they stood.

They followed him for about ten minutes and in that time passed more faces than they'd ever seen in their lives. A frenetic stream of horse-drawn carts and people came rushing down the narrow street. They passed a young man unloading wooden crates off a cart. They stared in innocent surprise, for he had skin that was dark, a shade they'd never before seen on a person. But they could not dawdle—their guide was still moving upstream, against the crushing current. The city sent up a din—a rumbling of carriage wheels, the shuffling of shoes on cobbles, a mangy dog barking—and here, by a street corner, a rail thin man shouting at the top of his lungs, holding out newspapers. Whatever it was to make this man holler, the news was portentous and dire. Hearing him go on worried the children, as did the jostling of bodies around them, and the speed with which dusk was approaching. The shadows in the long street were deep, darkening, and the old man was slowing down.

Upon reaching a lamp post, he rested against it. He was short of breath. Though the evening was cold, his face was damp with perspiration. He pointed with a trembling finger up the street as Ona and Lukas came near. He gestured emphatically, then pushed them gently on. He wanted them to continue without him. Perhaps he was tired. Perhaps he'd gone as far as he was able or willing, and now they would be on their own.

Their steps were hesitant. They didn't know where to direct their gaze. At the street, littered with trash and dung? At the windows glinting overhead? Or the signs over storefronts, painted in garish colors? And then there were the faces blurring by, stern with purpose, their eyes bright with fear. But fear of what? Of what malice? What villains or monsters? And if those who knew these streets were fearful, what ought these children feel?

Soon the street branched in two directions. They stopped and looked across the intersection. Nearby, another young man was shouting at the passersby, hawking newspapers. Perhaps because he looked not much older than Ona herself, and because a boy who sold news must be in the business of knowing things, Ona went to him and, in her clumsy Russian, asked where to find Henry Street, as she pointed at the address beneath Lukas' drawing.

He stared at her coldly, glanced at the address, at her brother, and then again at the paper. Then, understanding, he pointed up to the right and then the left.

Ona thanked the boy and led Lukas to the right, rushing across the street as fast she could, to avoid a cart coming quickly down the crossroad. They passed there a man dressed all in black, holding in his hand a pocket watch, eyeing it closely. Somewhere nearby, raucous church bells rang out the hour, a flock of pigeons careened overhead, and the man with the watch nodded at Ona, as if granting her permission to proceed down the dark street.

Snow began to gently fall on all who passed. It was quieter here with fewer people about, though near a stoop, a gang of pale boys had gathered. They talked sullenly among themselves, keeping watch. One called out to Ona and Lukas, causing the others to laugh, so that the children hurried by to get past their jeers.

They came to a crossing and stopped to look all four ways. In each direction, the streets stretched long distances. Behind them, the boys' laughter rang out. One of them came into the street to hurl a rock in their direction. It nearly hit Lukas in the head.

—Hurry, said Ona pulling her brother to the left. They rushed down the short block and there, on the next corner, on a sign nailed to the wall, they saw the words they'd been looking for all along: *Henry Street*. Lukas gave a cry, pointing at the sign. At last, they knew they were near.

Henry Street was ghostly. The snow made it so, and the shadows. A tall black horse, snorting clouds of breath, dragged a cart with a coffin in its bed. The hooves clacked on the cobbles, the cart groaned and rattled. The driver looked drowsy at the reins. The children watched him go by. On a balcony above the street, a large dog stood and howled. An old man strolled by muttering in what the children knew to be Yiddish. Streetlights flared along the way, and windows burned with strange electric light.

They soon found the building, the very address their mother had used in her letters. It was all brick, shrouded in darkness, five stories tall. Their mother's room, they knew from her letters, would be on the fourth floor, and so they entered the dank stairwell and climbed. It smelled of cooking. Somewhere a woman was singing behind a closed door.

On the fourth floor, they found four doors, and though it was nearly pitch dark on the landing, they could make out the very faint sheen of brass numbers. Only one matched the address in their mother's letters. Standing before it, Ona began to cry with relief and fatigue and fear—fear that they'd come to the wrong door, the wrong building, the wrong city altogether, for was it not possible that their mother had moved on, vanished into distant reaches of this country like their father?

Lukas banged at the door, calling in his bright voice:

—Mamytė!

Then he waited. No one came. Lukas knocked again, more gently now, until they heard a voice—thin, female—come from behind the door. A bolt slid open, a lock clicked, and then a blade of light fell upon them. Marija, their mother's cousin, appeared on the threshold. She gave a cry and leaped out to wrap them up in her arms, calling out their names, kissing the tops of their heads.

—Jesus, Jesus, my children. How did you get here? Come inside!

She ushered them into a little room, a kitchen with a heavy iron stove. Marija wore only a nightgown, and her hair looked as if she'd just come from bed. She was a tall, frail woman with a sickly pallor. She said she couldn't believe her eyes—were Karolina's children really here, in New York?

—Yes, but where is Mamytė? asked Lukas.

Her face fell. She opened her mouth, then closed it again.

—We've been very ill, she said. I was making tea when you knocked.

They all looked at the kettle steaming on the stove, on the brink of boiling.
   —The fool, she went out in the cold two days ago to buy chamomile and came back sick. She's been in and out of sleep ever since.
   Marija gestured to a door. Lukas rushed to open it, just as the kettle screeched.

Her children were calling.
   Karolina knew their voices. Had known them all along, even before they'd been born. The high, bright voice—it belonged to her son. The quiet one, to her daughter. She knew them. Yet the conviction fell squarely upon her:
   I have died.
   And death was like losing something once clung to as precious and realizing the treasure had been nothing at all. The parting of life fell as lightly as snow. It was a matter of course. All partings were. It would be no trouble now to get up and walk into the forest where she knew her parents to be. They would feed her the mushrooms she'd gathered, and so the timeless time of her death would begin.
   Yet she heard her boy calling, insistent, a warm commotion nearby. She could hear Marija saying her the

names of her children. At first, she thought, they have come to say goodbye; they know that I am dead. But then, with an inward chill, the truth surfaced in her: all this tumult was life. Life made this ruckus, and life called her name: *Mamytė, Mamytė...*

In the years between then and her true death, Karolina would sometimes wonder where God had been. Perhaps in the faces of those she'd passed in the street on the way to buy chamomile, or in the flowers themselves, or her very own legs that carried her across the island. Yet what felt most God-like and lasting was the conviction that she had died. It spread through her, a warmth of knowing. She would no longer fear. She felt free, released of all burdens into boundless woods and peace.

When the door opened, and her children came upon her, joy sliced into her like a knife. Life rushed in. Her ears filled with the sound of her own hot blood. Her children threw their arms around her neck, calling *Mamytė, Mamytė*—the word familiar yet newly strange.

She opened her eyes and saw them. She touched her daughter's pale hands, brushed them against her own face. Above them, on the ceiling, a crack made the jagged line of a continent or sea on a map. The Merkys and its forests were nowhere near. She was in New York, a city of cracked buildings, piled high with death and dying.

Her cousin Marija appeared. She hovered over the bed, holding in her hands a cup of steaming tea. She handed it to Karolina, who breathed in its delicate floral scent, remembering the woman in mourning attire and the man who'd followed her with his watch. These sensations seemed distant now; they belonged to another country and era, as if she had crossed an ocean of time to take this warm cup in her hands.

Her daughter wanted to know if she was okay, if she was glad to see them, happy that they had come at last. The girl's face was wet of tears. So was the boy's as he reached up to give Karolina a hot-mouthed kiss. The scent of home, after all those miles, was still on his body.

The years stretched out before her. She would yet grow old. Her children would. Karolina held the cup to her lips and sipped.

Acknowledgments

While writing this book, I benefited from the good sense and camaraderie of John Barry, Mikita Brottman, and Saul Myers. An early excerpt from the story appeared in *The Museum of Americana*, and I thank its prose editor Lauren Alwan. In describing Karolina's "atlas", I consulted recipes contained within *Polish Herbs, Flowers & Folk Medicine* by Sophie Hodorowicz Knab (Hippocrene Books, 1999). I am also grateful to Michelle Ross and the readers and staff who contributed their time and energy to the Stillhouse Press novella project, especially Linda Hall. Finally, I thank Solveiga, who first introduced me to the forests of southern Lithuania, and my children: Lukas for his illustrations, Dainora for her thoughtful attention to the manuscript, and both of them for their good cheer and love.

About the Author

Paul Jaskunas is the author of the novel *Hidden* (Free Press, 2004), which won the Friends of American Writers Award, and of *Mother Ship*, a poetry chapbook forthcoming from Finishing Line Press. His writing has appeared in the *New York Times, America, Tab: The Journal of Poetry & Poetics*, and *The Vilnius Review*, among many other publications. Since 2008, he has taught literature and writing at the Maryland Institute College of Art in Baltimore, where he edits *Full Bleed*, an annual journal devoted to the intersection of the visual and literary arts.